OUT OF REVENGE

BY

K S MICHAELS

Part 2 of the *Out Of Justice* Series

Prologue;

Caroline drove for a few hundred more miles, thinking solely of her predicament.
Having spoken to her mother and found that she was safe helped immensely with her
stress level.   Having spoken with her husband Jack, however, managed to stir up a great
deal of new emotions deep in her gut.   Knowing he had protected her back surely made her feel
safer.   That he knew her every move, made her only miss him more since her
last communication with him.   She knew that deep down, he meant no harm to her and
El.   It wasn't his way.   But it wasn't her way to live with the dangers and illegal
activities that he and his family were involved in.   It wasn't an acceptable life-choice for
her.   The horrors that she witnessed that day in the living room of that small family
would stay engraved in her mind for the rest of her life.   She was an idealist with notions
of white picket fences, freshly mowed lawns, where neighbors wave hello and no one is
transporting dead bodies while they chemically decompose in barrels at the local
self-storage facility.

Her long drive with El took her clear across the country until the road ran out at
the beaches of Florida.   With her mind adrift, she probably could have driven around the
entire globe without noticing, had she not run out of land.   Perhaps it was fate or irony, it was anyone's
guess as to why she chose to stay in Florida.   Only Caroline knew the truth
behind her decision to stay there.

Arrangements were made and identities were changed once again.   In less than a
week, El was back in school, and Caroline found a job working at a real estate office
by the marina.   The rent was much more expensive in this area, but at least, the
sales' commissions could be equally handsome and would suffice quite nicely.

Staying in West Palm Beach, Florida became the girl's new norm.   While
working in the real estate business, Caroline was becoming more familiar with the area.
She found Jack's previous beach house.   Seeing it in person, made her understand just
how much he was giving up to move to California to be with her.   The place was no less
than a stately mansion.   Seeing the house seemed to bring her closer to his past.
In a small way, she felt a tie between them, having found so much of his past.   In a less
visceral way, she felt a connection with Jack as she familiarized herself with his old
town.   Though he wouldn't be with her as she visited the local eateries and such, he
was a spiritual presence just the same.   It wasn't an easy choice for her to make, dealing with the absence of her husband, knowing he was just a simple phone call away.
But her principals and virtues would be, forever, in question if she were to go back to
him.   And yet, he was her only desire.

It came as a sudden surprise to receive the text from Crystal on her cell
phone one afternoon.   The message read: It's me, Crystal. Please pick up! A second

later, the phone rang with Crystal's voice on the other end.   Caroline never would have
thought she would ever hear her voice again.   The reasons for the phone call were brief,
to the point and mildly poignant.   She wanted Caroline to know how much respect she had for the choices she had made, and the endurance she had prevailed.   On the other hand, she wanted Caroline to know that she was fully aware of the family business and that she was perfectly comfortable knowing she would be safe and secure at home with her family. She also wanted her to understand how much Jack desired to be honest with her from the start, but couldn't risk losing her.   She described the love he still held for her, and Crystal gave many reasons for her to come back.   It was obvious that the family loved her, and didn't blame her for leaving.   But the phone call was with bias, and less understanding of Caroline's inner feelings and principal's of the matter.   Crystal missed her new sister in law, and understood the confusion that she faced.   She also wanted her to know that the family would always be safer when together at home.   The seed of thought had been planted.   If nothing else, Crystal had given her an out if ever
she might choose to come home.

        After careful consideration and a lot of self-flogging, Caroline initiated a weekly
phone call between Jack and his daughter.   It was the least she could do considering how
they missed each other.   There was no hiding from him, that was evident. Caroline reasoned surely no harm would come to them via a weekly phone call.

        On El's seventh birthday, Caroline had made a visitation to California.

Jack could not have been more happy to see the girls. A warm welcoming party was eventually assembled to greet them both.   Perhaps, the seed of thought that Crystal planted, had done some growing over the months.   Perhaps, being the wife of a hit-man would simply take some getting used to.

Chapter One
One year before El's seventh birthday.

Chapter Two
Life or death

Chapter Three
Recovery time

Chapter Four
The dangers of complacency

Chapter Five
The break in

Chapter Six
Gang relations

Chapter Seven
The investigation

Chapter Eight
Comfort in being on the road

Chapter Nine
Taking care of business

Chapter Ten
Business as usual

Chapter Eleven
Road trip

Chapter Twelve
Florence 86 Boys

Chapter Thirteen
Anticipation

Chapter Fourteen
Endometrial Malignancy

Chapter Fifteen
Making arrangements

Chapter Sixteen
Travel arrangements

Chapter Seventeen
Unfavorable tidings

Chapter Eighteen
Her first vision

Chapter Nineteen
Crystal's arrival

Chapter Twenty
The will to live.

Chapter Twenty-one
The reckoning.

Chapter Twenty-two
The challenge of instincts

Chapter twenty-three
Out of revenge

Chapter Twenty-four

Warfare

Chapter Twenty-five
Perdition

Chapter Twenty-six
Recovery

Part II -- 'Out of Range'
Chapter Twenty-seven
Training

Chapter One
One year before El's seventh birthday.

       The conversastion with Jack continued to ring in Caroline's ears for several weeks.   She never realized that he had kept tabs on her the entire time. Nore did she find out that Jack and his crew intentionally burned the house to the ground once all evidence of her and El's existence was wiped clean. Still playing the guardian of all her moves, Jack would continue to keep a protective vigil over his girls.   With every passing day of their separation, Jack was missing his wife more, and falling deeper in love with his lovely counterpart.   All that he had left in his heart of solidarity was a hope and a dream that Caroline would soon come back to him.   Instead of being the man who might make demands upon her, and obtrusively enforce his life style in her face, Jack gave her the space she needed to think.   He allotted her all the time she might require to think things through, all in hope that she would re-evaluate, reconsider and promptly return.   His plan was simple yet, admirable in her eyes as well.   However, his earnest kindness and understanding made things more difficult for Caroline, as apposed to Jack having been angered and insistent upon the girls' returning. It would have been so much easier on her discition making had he been an ass and had his crew kidnap her, and bring her back by physical force.   No doubt, he had the power and the recourses to do so. And it would have been so much easier to put out the order for her return.   But he knew that kind of action would have been futile in matters of the heart. Instead, Jack was everything Caroline had fallen in love with.   Granted he had made the most vital mistake from the very start by not having been perfectly honest with her.   But he had made that choice based upon his insight of her steadfast virtues. He couldn't blame her for how things unfurled leading to their separation.   She had warned him from the start, honesty was her first and primary rule of marriage.

Two weeks after Caroline and El found a new place to rent, Jack continued to work at his plan to win his wife over with kindness and the healing properties of time.   Now that Caroline understood the truth that she would never be able to elude her doting husband with his endless resources and his stoutworthy survalance over her, he sent her and El an unmarked care package addressed to Gertrude who goes by Agness.   Jack had saved them the effort of going through unsecured avenues for the task of new identities.   One way of guaranteeing his girls' safety would be to use his own people for the job of creating the fake identification.   To her surprise, he had included a concealed weapons permit (CCW) matching the new name of her identification. Listed on the CCW license were three handguns to add to her arsenal.   However, she didn't know why Jack would send her a CCW without showing her how to go about matching serial numbers on three new guns.   It wouldn't be until the following day, another box arrived at her new home.   Enclosed were the brand new guns already licensed to her, matching the already registered serial numbers.   The second box had inadvertently been delayed by some unforeseen mishap.   Jack had thought of everything, accept the incidental, everyday unfortunate lag via the United Postal Service.   The added measurers of precautions that Jack had taken made good sense, but also had elevated a great deal of stress on everyone involved.   In addition to the guns, he had enclosed cash to help offset some of the expenditures of

Caroline's new move.   No doubt, building a hidden safe room and purchasing all new furniture would be a costly expendeture.   However, the twenty-five thousand dollars that Jack sent was a bit overkill. But that was Jack's way.   His doting love and admiration for his wife held no bounds.   The man was very much in love with his wife, and there would be no way to change that.

Once Caroline had procured a good home in a safe neighborhood, she was fast at work, building all the necessary security features needed to ensure a safe environment for herself and El.   With the windfall of CCW, she purchased a new Mossberg shotgun to be hidden in the home while either one of the other three guns would be strategically carried on her person, or hidden in her vehicle.   Of course, the rule of CCW explicitly defines the rules of concealment; at no time is hiding a gun in your car a legal act in accordance with the CCW parameters. The gun , or guns of concealment must be on your person in order to be within the letter of the laws provided for CCW carriers.   However, Caroline was very good at hiding guns, and believed it was better to be alive than the sorry alternative. The rule of thumb is, and always has been; "It is far better to be tried by 12 than carried by 6."   No sooner Caroline got the Mossberg home, she removed the stock butt of the gun and replaced it with a pistol grip.   She shortened up the barrel using the optional one provided in the kit.   With the length of the shotgun reduced by nearly half, after the alterations, she was assured the ability to manouver with better accuracy should she encounter oposition at close range.   Even with light bird shot loaded in the shotgun, the effect would be deadly without the need for perfect accuracy.   No doubt, Caroline was learning the ropes of her weaponry.   Having already experienced one very freighting and deadly gun battle, she had a very good idea as to what arsenal would be best suit her needs should another gunfight ensue at close quarters.   Under desquise, Caroline would make many trips to the firing range to help improve upon her shooting skills.   Florida was nothing like the desert of her last residence.   There were fewer places she could run off to   and shoot freely at a mountainside.   Thankfully, her clever disquise added a good cloak of protection to her identity via her anonymity.   Though the shooting range of her choice required monthly membership, Caroline didn't mind as long as she knew her identity was well concealed.   And fortunately, the club that she attended, valued their member's privacy.

After the first day in Florida, it was obvious to Caroline that she would need to get rid of her old truck as soon as possible.   A truck in the desert, her past locale, was perfectly appropriate and overlooked, but in the ritzy neighborhood of West Palm Beach, her old truck would be as outspoken and as out of place as Woody Allen in a bikini contest. With the help of Jack's gracious cash gift, Caroline purchased a certified used Jaguar XJS.   Not only was the car more appropriate for her line of work, but she was able to make many unnoticeable changes to the wooden dashboard.   Using the very design that Jaguar prided beauty and elogance, Caroline modified the car with virtual perfection.   Only a trained eye might notice the changes that she had made.   From within the hidden privacy of her garage, Caroline was able to build a cache behind the dashboard from which she was able to hide several handguns.   At the ready, she could make easy work of unlocking the latch that kept the guns concealed. Her craftsman's skills were improving each time her task would present new challenges.   She was a wiz with carpentry.   The compliment of her skills would bleed from her real estate sales and back to her private life.   Time and time again, she worked hand in hand with many of her clients and contractors in order to make certain and conditional sales at her place of work.   She advanced her undesrtanding of construction to the point where she was able to aid many of her clients with helpful hints and money saving opportunities.   It didn't take long before she became a valuable asset at her new position as a real estate agent.   Soon, many of her coworkers were taking her advise and skills as virtual gospel.

The life of a single mother working as a real-estate agent in a predominantly wealthy environment gave way to an entirely new realm which was to remain concealed from the past, seemed to be working well.   The first few months of looking over her shoulder and keeping vigil over every passing car was the worst of her paranoid aggression.   But, eventually, her worrisome anxiety would slow from a full-on boil to a tepid simmer.

El took well to her new school and environment as well.   Being a clever girl with advanced academic skills in the Gate Program, the misfortune of moving from place to place didn't effect her in any adverse way.   Though the challenge of changing one's name and address so often, was a bit of a hindrance for such a young mind of six years old, El quickly adjusted well to her state of change.   Sadly, the effort that Caroline would make at subsiding the urge to see Daddy, would fall on deaf ears.   El would continue to pressure Mom to make the effort to see Daddy at every given chance. It was hard on the both of them, but it became especially hard on Caroline when the temptation and nagging needs would urge her along as well.   Each week, El would speak to her daddy over the phone.

And each week, Caroline would hear Jack's voice over the speaker.   The temptation to give-in would always play havoc with Caroline's libido.   She missed him terribly.   Had it not been for her ability to drown her emotions into her work, she, no doubt, might have dropped everything long before, to be back at Jack's side.   Caroline used all her energies to make her profession a successful one.   No one at her company invested the long hours of work that she did.   Though one might have believed she was primarily interested in making millions of dollars, it was so not the truth.   The subterfuge was for the benefit of easing her own mind.   She made herself into a working machine to keep from thinking about the man she missed so much.   So many times, she thought how much easier it all would have been if Jack was a misogynistic bastard.

It had only been sixty three days since the girls first arrived in West Palm Beach.   They were well settled in.   El was already achieving academic awards for her efforts, and Caroline was raking in some very sizable commissions.   Her name was already becoming a reference among those looking to buy or sell a home.   Though it was inevitable, the big question came up when Caroline's broker named Fred Niedrickson would finally ask why she would refuse to show her photo in the weekly sales magazines.   All the other ladies in the office were only too happy to have their glamour shots posted in the magazines in hope to boost sales.   Innocent enough was the question of curiosity that came from Fred who also added that she was very pretty. Evidently, he might have thought that she felt she wasn't pretty enough to be presented along side the properties for sale.   Caroline simply explained that she had been attacked by a man once while showing a house in California.   She claimed that she believed that the attacker had picked her based upon her photograph in a magazine.   Fortunately, after that answer, Fred would never bother her with personal questions of her private life or her reasons for her certain idiosyncrasies.   As long as he was getting his three percent commissions from her sales, he was ecstatic with her success and dedication to the business.   Fred was a reasonable man in his late sixties.   He ran a respectable business, and valued his agents.   He had a family of his own with grandkids that he rarely got to see due to the fact that all his kids lived on the West coast.

One Friday, Caroline was working late in the office.   She had a great deal of paperwork to catch up on.   It was not unusual for Caroline to, occasionally, pick El up from school and bring her back to the office.   Many times, El would be found working on her school work along side her mother looking like a mini real estate agent busy behind the desk.   Caroline had extra space in her office dedicated just for her adorable little daughter.   After the first time Fred met little El, he had decided to call her Little Miss. The cute name just seemed to suit her perfectly.   With long black curly hair and adorable dimples on both cheeks, Little Miss was a charming addition to the company.   After that day, the name simply stuck.   El was proud of her new name, feeling professional and one of the crew.   It was less than a week after Fred first met Little Miss when he had a custom sports jacket made for her.   The jacket represented the gold and black colors of the agency. On one side of the jacket, just beneath the lapel and above the pocket was the name of the agency.   On the other side was a name label reading Little Miss. One might have thought the young little tyke had won the Toys R Us lottery when Fred presented her

with her own work jacket.   Proudly, from that day
forward Little Miss made sure to dress into her jacket
the minute she stepped into the office.   To add some
prestige to the hype of her excitement, Fred had
given Little Miss some chores to do once her
homework was done.   Among the list of things to do
around the office was stocking the coffee filters, light
sweeping of the floors, loading paper in the copier
tray and a few other miscellaneous things that Little
Miss would take pride in doing.   Each day after
finishing with her schoolwork, she rushed to get
started with the privilege of being seen in public
working along side the adults in the office.   The
young lady got a kick out of the comments she got
from the clients that came in the door.   At the end of
the week, Fred took great pleasure in presenting
Little Miss with gifts of his gratitude for work well
done.   Since Fred couldn't spoil his own grandkids,
he took great pride in spoiling Little Miss.   Of
course, Caroline would insist that payment was not
necessary, Fred refused to listen.   Seeing the little
girl's look of excitement each week seemed to be
something he looked forward to just as much as Little
Miss.

        As Caroline worked at her desk, attempting to
finalize some forms at the close of an escrow on one
of her sales for that week, the phone rang out echoing
throughout the empty building.   She answered the
call to hear a young man asking for one of the other
agents.   However, the lady he requested to speak
with was out for the weekend and would not be
returning until Monday.   Generally, the policy in the
office would be to take the client's name and number
and have the agent call them back as soon as
possible.   Unfortunately, this guy was in to much of
a hurry to see a particular property that had just been
listed for the first day.   There are a great many

investors out in the field who pride themselves at being the very person to see a property and decide if it is something they would like to invest in or flip. The man on the other end of the phone seemed to be one of those guys who habitually insisted on being the first to check out beach property.   He claimed to have nearly a dozen rentals on the beach, and was still in search of more.   The man who introduced himself as Bob Smith insisted Caroline or someone else in the office show him the property that evening. Inasmuch as Caroline was the only one in the office, she made an effort to accommodate the man.   She scheduled the appointment, allowing herself just enough time to drop El off with the new Nanny and meet Bob Smith at the property.   In the business of real estate, the only money to be made is through commissions.   If Caroline didn't make any sales on any particular week, she and El would be without a paycheck that week.   Needless to say, sales were the lifeblood of business.   In an effort to please the client that evening, Caroline made herself available to show the beachfront property to Bob Smith.   Just as the Multiple Listing Service (MLS) had advertised, the house had just gone on the market that day.   One hour, to the minute, after the initial phone call, Caroline pulled up onto the driveway of the property.   Already there to greet her was a young man in his late twenties, standing next to his older model Mercedes Benz off to the side of the street at curbside.   The house was dark and secured with a lock box on the front door knob.   After introducing herself, Caroline opened the lock box, retrieved the key, and invited the man to join her inside the house. The man seemed very interested in the property just as he seemed over the phone.   Once inside, Caroline flipped every light switch she could find to light up the house, giving it a brighter, larger appearance.

The place came to life as the lights of chandeliers, sconces and accents showed brilliance throughout the house. Typical of many of the local houses in the area so close to the beach, were the hardwood floors and ceramic tiled floors. Carpet was never a good choice to have when beach-sand would be so hard to remove. As a result of the flooring, the high beamed ceilings and the lack of furniture, the house seemed to have an acoustic echo that bounced off every surface of the house. Caroline found the effect to be perfectly normal, however, the man seemed to be rather bothered by the racket the echo caused. As the two went to the back of the house to view the rooms, Bob showed vague interest in things most people with his investment interests would find very important. As they entered the second room, Bob never bothered to open the walk-in closet to check on it's size, something nearly everyone would do simply out of habit or simple interest. Leaving that room, Bob shut out the light behind them as he did after leaving the other room. After viewing the third and final bedroom, Bob asked about the price of the home. A sudden feeling of doubt seemed to strike a nerve with Caroline. The man hadn't even seen the kitchen, and already he was asking about the price. But the part that made little sense to Caroline was the fact that he intended to rent the property to summer visitors, yet, the man never bothered to check the view of the beach from the back yard. As Caroline made an attempt to show the man the kitchen, he seemed too hasty to be a seriously motivated buyer. She had enough experience to know when someone was a serious buyer, or just a lookyloo bent on wasting other people's time. Sensing the man was just a talker, Caroline resigned herself to the fact that he probably had little money enough to afford the eight-hundred thousand dollar home.   Perhaps, he only wanted to know what such a home might look like from the inside.   The simple fact remained, her sharp instincts were telling her, the man had little interest in buying the house.   It didn't take long before the guy showed nerve enough to compliment Caroline's appearance.   Without giving it much thought, she realized this guy probably got his kicks making business girls believe he was rich. His ploy was ineffective as she tried to keep his mind off of her and on the house.   His comment, as far as she was concerned was very inappropriate. Especially since she was still wearing Jack's wedding ring on her finger.   With every effort to continue with the tour of the house, the more Bob would resist her professional efforts and continued trying to make personal conversation.

"I thank you for the compliment, Bob, however, I am happily married with a family. Would you like to see the back deck and built-in rock barbeque?   I understand the owners held large parties on the deck that could accommodate a large number of people, perhaps for a wedding or other celebrations…"   Caroline tried to keep his mind off of her breasts and on business at hand by buttoning her jacket.   "As rental property, the deck could be the clincher with many renters."

Bob smiled showing little interest in what Caroline was saying and continued making his inappropriate comments.   "I love parties.   How would you like to go to a party with me tonight?   I know were there is rockin' party happening not far from here."

Caroline looked Bob dead in the eyes making every attempt to make her point clear.   "As I mentioned before, Mr. Smith, I am married…faithfully.   If you wish me to continue with the tour, I will be happy to do so, but I must insist you stop asking these inappropriate questions because, quite frankly, you are making me fell very uncomfortable."

Bob, stepped back showing a relenting pause in his approach. "I am sorry.   I shouldn't have come on like such a fool.   I don't know what came over me.   I guess it must have been your amazing body or something along those lines that got me going."   His cow-eyed stare with mouth agape continued as he spoke outright.

With Caroline having given the creepy guy every opportunity to make good of his personality, she made the decision to conclude the tour and hope he would not file a formal complaint against her as would happen so many times when some of the female agents would refuse the advancements of potential clients.   "Perhaps during the light of day, the house would have better appeal.   We have a number of agents that would make themselves available to you tomorrow or even on Sunday if you prefer.   I realize it is probably too dark for you to see the back deck anyhow."   Making any reasonable excuse to leave the creepy guy and his ugly advancements, Caroline headed toward the front door.

"I never said you could leave, bitch."   The stunning words hit like a wrecking ball   to her gut. His voice was no longer the insipid little frail sounding man that he conveyed before.

Chapter Two
Life or death

Caroline suddenly understood with total clarity what was to come in a an instant.   The throttling tug at the back of her head and neck proved his horrid intentions.   He grabbed at her long hair that was tied into a pony tail at mid back length. With unforeseen power, Bob had slammed her to the ground by pulling her by the hair with unrelenting force.   She landed hard onto the solid flooring with a crashing blow to her spine.   The twisting of her neck grinded with pops and crackles of every cervical vertebrae from he shoulders clear up to her head.   A shocking electrical pain shot through her body as though she had been electrocuted.   With the wind knocked out of her and her neck in agonizing pain, she feared she might have become paralyzed when she couldn't move her limbs to defend herself.

In an instant, Bob pounced his two-hundred pond frame against her body as he laid himself onto her.   His breath and odor was detected as foul and disgusting.

Immediately, Caroline remembered hearing about the news reports about a sexual predator who had been terrorizing women across the Eastern coast. The last to be raped was a car saleswoman who went on a test drive with a man who never returned.   Her body was later found along side the freeway embankment three days later.   Though the DNA of her attacker was found at the scene and on her, no records existed on the killer.   The guy had eluded the detectives for nearly a year as he continued on his ugly killing spree.   Thirteen innocent women lost their lives in less than twelve months.   As Caroline laid helplessly beneath the weight of Bob's grotesque body, she could feel his excitement that had already grown hard and rigid as he pressed himself against her.   The initial collision against the hardwood flooring caused Caroline to become completely immobile.

Bob's brute force was more than she had expected.   Knowing she never should have turned her back to him, Bob had taken every opportunity to gain advantage over his   prey.   His horrific actions were an impulsive hedonistic reflex to her helplessness.   He thrived on her fearful, ineffective resistance.   With every passing second, he became more and more aggressive.   Bob was so caught up in his own moment of excitement he hadn't noticed that Caroline was slowly gaining back her composure.

Caroline made every attempt to steady her mind to keep from panicking.   This was not a man to reason with or try to bargain with.   She knew he would not stop until she was dead.   She felt his grotesque grind against her privates growing more rampant.   Knowing she was able to feel her lower extremities indicated that she probably hadn't broken her neck or severed her spine.   Slowly, she began to feel her fingertips come back to life.   It was a very slow progression of recovery as her hands were next to show signs of life as well.   By which time, Bob was advancing faster than she was recovering.   His grinding motion was paused only by the time it took him to pull at his trousers.   With his erection in full view, Bob pressed the weight of his body against Caroline's legs pinning her down.   He tugged at the belt of Caroline's slacks.   With a quick sweeping motion, he pulled the belt free, tossing it across the slippery waxed floor.   His next move was an attempt to unbutton her pants.

Caroline resisted by expanding her belly against the material keeping him from progressing. The answer to her resistance was met with a closed-fisted, crashing blow to her jaw.   It wasn't the first time she had been throttled by a man of power.   The effect of such paralyzing horrors was an most alarming.   As her heart raced in her chest, as a flurry of vertigo overtook her.   The explosive fear for her life immediately caused an overpowering sensation of nausea. With every effort of her being she did her best to stay conscious.   With Bob holding himself up with one arm firmly planted on the floor, the other was feverishly pulling at the buttons of her pants. Having suddenly given away, the threads of the two buttons were forcefully torn away as the little plastic buttons tapped and bounced across the floor to a taper of silence.   The zipper of her pants gave little to no resistance as Bob pulled her pants down to her knees. With one simple tug, Bob had torn away her panties revealing her privates to him.   Caroline's mind was a flurry of images starting with the young innocents of El and ending with her need for Jack's help as she struggled to stay awake and alert.   She made every attempt to muster the strength to keep this violent pig from taking what was prized to her.   She called upon her utmost anger and adrenalin to aid her resistance.   Unbeknown to most, Caroline's pretty painted fingernails had little to do with esthetics and femininity.   With the aid of Gelatin tablets taken before bed each night to strengthen her fingernails and with several coats of paint added to her nails,

Caroline would always be prepared with God given
weapons should her gun be too far from reach.
With all the energy that she had left in her little body,
she made good use of an open opportunity.   When
Bob was busy trying to guide himself into her,
Caroline reached for his face.   She grasped both
sides of his face and made use of every bit of strength
she could call upon to gouged into his eyes using
both her thumb nails.   In an instant, Bob wriggled
his weight off of her in an attempt to escape the
intense pain she had inflicted upon him.   Shaky and
still off balance, Caroline crawled to her purse that
had fallen by the front door.   As Bob groaned and
gasped out of anger and pain, Caroline quickly
located her cell phone and dialed 911.
        "Yes, this is an emergency.   I am at--"
Caroline was stunned to learn she had been put on
hold.
        Now, after hearing Caroline's voice and a
partial conversation, Bob was fully aware of what his
latest victim was attempting to do.   There was no
way in his mind, she could be allowed to escape his
wrath.   Hitherto, she was the only one who could
identify him.   Aside from his method of operation,
the cops had yet to find one single lead or shred of
evidence on this evil man.   It was entirely up to
Caroline to make good on his capture and arrest.
"You fucking bitch.   You nearly punctured my
eyes…"   Bob shouted angrily as he made an
attempt to open his eyes in order to find her.
        Knowing she was still much too weak to
stand and open the front door, Caroline made every
attempt to quietly scoot herself away from his reach.
Using a pen she found in her purse, she threw it
across the room hoping he would follow the sound
away from her.   Unfortunately, Bob had partial
vision in one eye, defeating her ploy.

With rains of tears pouring from both his eyes, Bob walked on his knees with his left arm protruding forward towards Caroline.   For a portly man in pour physical shape, he seemed to move rather quickly.   Even with his pants still around is knees, he was about to gain ground on Caroline's futile attempt to escape.   "Get over here, you slutty piece of shit."   His vulgar words shot angry fear through her very soul.

Her body was still in the state of shock.   Her mental faculties were fully intact, however, her physical was in complete shambles.   Whatever damage that had been caused by the explosive, unsuspecting jerking of her neck and the fall onto her back caused her to lose nearly eighty-five percent of her motor skills.   Had she, at least, another ten percent of her strength, she no doubt, would have been able to puncture both his eye balls in the sockets closing in on the odds of survival.   Which, of course, was her intent from the very start.   She knew who this guy was; the caliber of his personality was all-telling from the start.   And had she listened to her instincts, she never would have turned her back to this guy.   There was no doubt in her mind that this guy was the East Coast Strangler.   Unfortunately, her strength was inhibited by the palsied unsteadiness of her nervous system.   She had to keep her wits about her just to stay conscious.   The inhibiting vertigo and the pounding migraine that soon developed would have made it easy for her to lay down and pass out, but her daughter, El would no longer have had a mother to raise her.   And that was not going to be an option.   Fighting to stay awake, Caroline used the bare skin of her sweaty palm to gain traction on the hardwood floors.   Pulling her unresponsive body across the floor using elbows and flesh, she made every attempt to move from Bob's encroaching attack.   The amount of time she was placed on hold by the 911 operator seemed like an eternity.   Having to hold the phone in one hand and crawl with the other made in virtually impossible for her to effectively escape his grasp.

"It's bitches like you that give fancy homes like this a bad name.   Too high and mighty to be friends with the lower class.   All you bitches care about is the rich dick."   Bob made his point clear as he got hold of Caroline's ankle.   He pulled her closer to his harbor as her skin squealed and burned from the dragging friction of the flooring.   "Dead or alive, I'm getting what I came for, bitch."   His disgusting manner and view on life was as repulsive as his ignorant comments.   The moment he had Caroline beneath him once, again, his misguided sexual drive worked feverishly at his libido. Though he had trouble seeing, he had no difficulty finding his groping way along Caroline's half naked body.   As if he were climbing a rope, he pulled her by her left ankle and then her bare skinned thigh. He groped at her privates, and prepared to steady himself once more at her haunches.   As he regained his erection, he paid little attention to Caroline's struggle.

With exponential succession, Caroline had gained back enough strength, finally, to protect herself from any more of his advancements.   He was so caught up in the moment of self gratification, he hardly noticed Caroline had retrieved her handgun. With one crashing blow to his left temple, she slammed the butt of her handgun against the side of his head.   Aiming for the temple, she hit target, dead on.   Bob fell over like a sack potatoes shacking the floor beneath them both.   She had managed to retrieved her pistol that was holstered at her right ankle.   It wasn't until the very last moment, was she able to unsnap the strap that held her weapon in place, and bend her knee within reach.   As yet, Caroline hadn't the strength or composure to escape from the house.   But fortunately, as if to be hearing the cavalry horn, the 911 operator came back on line. "Thank God."   Caroline exasperated.   "The East Coast Strangler has just attacked me…oh God no…" Caroline was shocked to see Bob back on his knees, attempting to right himself and approach her once again.   As grotesque as all that she could imagine, Bob was obviously excited by her struggle to survive his wrath.   His steady erection was evident as was his intention to grab the phone from her.   Though Caroline couldn't hear what the operator was saying, Caroline was quite certain the operator would be able to hear her end of the conversation quite clearly. With one sweeping motion, Caroline slid the cell phone away from the both of them.   Far enough from Bob's reach, yet close enough to record the events to follow.   "Get off of me."   Caroline shouted.

With the phone out of reach, Bob disregarded his attempt to retrieve it.   He had only one thing on his mind.   That fact that Caroline had a gun, didn't seem to impede him in the least.   "You stupid bitch. I already told you, dead or alive, I'm getting what I came for."   Bob was still wavering slightly from the blow he got to the temple.   And his aim was probably blurred from the damage she inflicted to his eyes.   Bob slammed his fist to the floor just missing Caroline's face.   The tempestuous impact was loud and reverberant, yet, Bob showed little effect from the pain he must have suffered.

Letting out a window-shattering scream, Caroline made sure the operator could hear her plea for life.   "Please don't kill me.   Just go away and I wont tell anyone…"

"Fuck you, bitch." Bob said, loud and clear as he readied himself to throw another punch to her face.

"No, *fuck you, bitch*." Caroline whispered, for his ears only. The loud report of the gunfire echoed through the house like a cannon. No doubt, her ears might have taken some temporary damage from such a loud blast at close range and with no ear protection.

Bob's blood had splattered all over her face and front. His limp body fell back upon his knees. With a bullet hole in his forehead, Caroline took no chances. She emptied the gun shooting the remaining six bullets into his chest. Bob slumped backwards after the last bullet found its way home at bull's-eye. As the body remained in a sitting position, Caroline struggled, freeing herself from beneath him and crawled across the floor. She had only enough strength left in her body to retrieve the phone and report the address of the house.

Remembering nothing else of the shooting event, Caroline was later admitted to the hospital. She had been taken by ambulance minutes after her 911 call found her location. The last thing Caroline needed was publicity and news reporters. Thankfully, Fred Niedrickson was alerted immediately after she was admitted to the hospital. Inasmuch as she was, in fact, on the job when the incident occurred, and it is hospital policy to call the employer first. Knowing that Caroline kept private and listed no next of kin on any of her paperwork, Fred respected her privacy and instructed the news crews to leave Agnes Pimpleton alone, or he would be calling the police. Which he did anyhow. As it turned out, Fred was quite a good friend to Caroline and Little Miss.

Agnes Pimpleton was a pet name that Caroline used for Little Miss anytime she might slip up and accidentally use her true name.   Somehow, the silliness of it caught on, and often used the name in the office as levity and silliness.

Soon, every channel on the television was boasting the latest news about the final end to the East Coast Strangler.   Had it not been for Fred's handy work and quick thinking, Caroline's face might have gone public along with the man who claimed to be Bob Smith.   Though the tenacious reporters insisted on seeing the heroine who stopped the ravages of a demented mind, the hospital did a good job keeping them away.   Plus, had it not been for Fred moving Caroline to a private hospital, things might have gone public, after all.   To her surprise, Fred more than simply understood Caroline's plea for anonymity.   Instinctively, he understood there was something deeper going on in her life.   And knowing how important her privacy was to her, he took action and moved her away from the public eye. He knew what would be best for his friend and employee.   And honoring her wishes, he knew what would be the right action to take.

For weeks the news reporters scrambled to find the girl who defended herself against the notorious killer.   It wouldn't be too long before, she and the public learned that he had killed far more women than first thought.   And just as she had suspected, his demented mind was everything she found him to be.   The frightening things he had said to her during his attack were founded and factual. Through the findings of an ongoing investigation and DNA research the sick bastard had, in fact, killed many of the women long before he had raped them. In one case, he had killed the victim with one blow to the face when he had first encountered her, then took her body to a secluded place were he had his way with her.   Her lifeless, already decaying, body was found by hikers several days after her death.   Nearly every news channel was covering the story with so called psychological specialist delving into the psychotic minds of the sick and afflicted. Necrophilia become the topic on the news for several grueling days to follow.   As hideous as it all may have seemed, Caroline and most of the public had come to learn that a larger number of sick minded individuals share a similar carnal drive for such horrific pleasures involving the dead or disabled.

Unlike most rape victims, Caroline lived to tell the story.   She reported all that she knew to the police from the very start.   Thankfully, her paperwork was all found to be in order and her true identity was never discovered.   And just as she had planned, the 911 tapes were reviewed and found to be a textbook case of self-defense in a life or death situation.

After spending only one night in the hospital that Fred had procured for her privacy, Caroline tested well.   She had suffered a sprained neck that would take nearly three months to heal.   With physical therapy and plenty of rest, the doctor projected a clean bill of health.   Thankfully, El was in good hands while Mom stayed in the hospital over night.   The new nanny that Caroline hired came highly recommended through one of the other girls in the office.   Once Caroline was back in the comfort of her own home, El was happy to have her mom back home.   While out on leave, the girls made plans together.   As long as Caroline was doing well, they would go shopping together and go on a few outings.   The girl-time spent together was very therapeutic for the both of them.

Chapter Three
Recovery time

Oddly, from the day Caroline and El moved form the desert to West Palm Beach, it seemed they had jumped from the kettle into the frying pan. Though she knew she needn't worry about Jack knowing were she lived, she did, however, find her situation with the L.A. gang very unnerving. Weekly reports from Jack would reach Caroline telling her of his ongoing investigation. Unfortunately, Jack wasn't getting much information. The gang kept very unorthodox ways.   Vendettas were kept secret, and information was especially hard to come by.   For the most part, Jack believed that the L.A. gang had no idea who or where Caroline was.   He reported that she had made a clean getaway and she had nothing to worry about. However, one underlying situation bothered her from the start.   Big Mike had an older brother who disappeared shortly after Big Mike's death.

Thankfully, Caroline's face never made headlines after the Bob Smith's death.   Though she was ready and able to leave town in an instant and slip away into the night without a trace, she wasn't necessarily willing to make that transition just yet. She wanted to play out the situation for as long as she could.   El was doing rather well in school, and work was actually quite profitable, and enjoyable.   To leave now would mean starting all over and battling with the rigors of change.   So far, she didn't see any signs of
problems from the gang of L.A.

During the three week recovery period that Caroline took from work, El and Caroline had a great deal of fun together, girl shopping and simply being together was minus the stress of being on the run. Certainly, the stress levels had tapered off drastically. But Caroline was always careful not to fall into the pattern of complacency.   Even Fred Niedrickson had helped further with her anonymity by never telling anyone in the office what had happened to Caroline, never revealing the fact that she was the one who stopped the East Coast Strangler.   With the house where the attack took place off the market, no one knew the better.   The owners didn't re-list the house for several months after the incident. Caroline's secret was safe, for the most part.

Three weeks after the attack, Caroline returned to work.   She still felt the residual aches and pains of her neck strain, but she seemed to feel better when her mind was busy and occupied with work.   Her excuse to the other workers at the office for taking off so much work was simply personal. And no one questioned it, thereafter.   Oddly, Caroline never thought much about Bob Smith and the justice she served to her community by eliminating such a horrible monster.   Had it not been for the injury she sustained by his cowardice act, she never would have had any trouble dealing with him at all.   Unlike Big Mike and his dedicated band of gang members, Bob was no real threat, and nothing more to worry about once the threat was gone.   Once the DNA found on many of the victims matched up with Bob Smith, the cops were reluctant to do much of a background check on Caroline. With all the work and trouble Jack had gone through to make certain her guns and licenses were clean, there were no red flags or suspicion giving anyone doubt or reason to search.   Within two weeks, after the close of the police investigation, Caroline was given back her gun.

As it was, Bob Smith was found to be a forty-year old single man, still living with his mother in her basement.   He was a high school dropout, who couldn't hold down a job longer than three months. His real name was Don McPoland.   There was an incident where Don had worked for a large utility company up until his employment was terminated due to his sexual advancements toward the ladies in the office.   Yet, for years, his mother believed he was a peaceful, traveling salesman.   According to her interview with the local news, she believed her son Don was a gentle and kind man who couldn't possibly have hurt the girls that they accused him of killing.   She vehemently denied his being involved with such a heinous crime, later stating the cops should be investigating and going after the murderer who killed *him*.   It was her belief that the true victim was her son who was probably robbed of his money and then killed.

Long after El had gone to bed, Caroline watched the news and witnessed the mother of Don McPoland go on and on about the innocence of her slain son.   Caroline wondered to herself how this woman would feel if she were able to see actual footage of her son committing   a crime.   Would she concede to the truth, or would she deny her own eyes and banter on about her son's good intentions. As far as what Caroline could see of the woman's mannerisms, she was probably an enabling mother who would back her child to the end regardless of the horrible crimes he had committed.   As she sat on the couch in front of the television growing more angry by the minute, the cell phone sitting next to her rang out.   To her surprise, it was Jack.   Understanding the call had to be important, she picked up the phone hoping there wasn't any bad news coming from his end.   One of Caroline's strict rule was that Jack not call her unless it was vitally important.

"Hello?"

"It's Jack, honey…everything is okay, however, I need to tell you that Big Mike's brother has been located.   And from what we have been able to learn, he's definitely looking for revenge for his brother's death.   The entire time he's been he was scouring the West coast pumping all his snitches and leads for information on you.   I have to tell you, I don't like the sound of it, Caroline.   He's a tough customer, this one."   Jack's earnest concern was obvious, as he tried to make the call as short as possible, detecting Caroline's hasty intentions.

"I'm ready for him."   Caroline showed little concern.   Her lack of concern seemed to be her way of hiding her stress.

"I know you are, babe.   I'm just concerned about you.   By the way, how's the neck?"   He asked, earnestly hoping she wasn't suffering.

"Still stiff, but the therapy is helping.   How's the family?"   She said, returning the perfunctory salutations.

"Everyone is fine, however Crystal has been under the weather for the past couple of weeks."

Hearing Crystals name made Caroline, suddenly, very homesick.   "What's wrong with her?"   She asked, sounding several tones less hasty.

"We all know how Crystal is with visiting doctors.   It may be a while before anyone can talk her into getting help."

"That's true.   Keep me informed, Jack.   I worry about her."   She instructed pragmatically.

"I will."   The pause of silence only lasted a second once Jack felt a loss of communication.

How's El?"

"You just spoke to her the other day, Jack. You know she's fine."   Caroline said in a reprimanding tone.

"Yeah, I know…I'm just…"   Jack couldn't find the words.

"We've been over this before, Jack.   We can't have these conversations.   It's too much too soon."   Knowing it was time to end the conversation before she was to break down in tears, she asked the last pertinent question.   "What is Big Mike's brother's name?"

"He goes by Little Chief, but his name is Al Rollins.   And he's not little."   Jack thought he might add his take on the oddity of the conundrum.

"I appreciate the heads up.   I will keep our daughter safe.   Tell Crystal I will be calling her once I change over to a new number."

"I can send you a--"   Jack was always trying to offer any assistance to help out at any cost.

"I got it.   Don't send any more.   You have been overly helpful already.   I have to do this on my own, Jack."   Adamantly, she braved the words knowing just how curt she was sounding.

"I understand.   Well, I better let you go now. I love you…"   Jack had a way of slipping those, three, words in just before the phone line would go dead.

Caroline pushed the end button on her phone just a half-second before she burst into tears.   Just hearing his voice gave her pains she never thought could hurt.   If it came down to a choice of missing Jack or facing Little Chief, Caroline would probably have picked to face Little Chief, ten times over. Missing Jack was a misery she dreaded on a daily basis.   Thankfully, El was fast asleep, allowing her the privacy to cry without restraint.   With her head buried in the muffle of the pillow, she stretched across the couch braying her heart out.   She needed this timeout.   It had been welling up inside her ever since the attack.   The tears poured and her face grew red and swollen as she gave that pillow all she had to surrender.   No matter how many times she tried not to say it, the words just seemed to come out through the tears, "I Love you too, Jack."   She probably would have braved it out for another month had she not heard Jack's voice over the phone.   So badly, she needed to crawl up into the harbor of his embrace and feel the safety of his protection.   Just thinking about him as she cried, brought on a new set of emotions.   She wanted to make love to him, but only after slapping him for having lied to her.   She wanted to tell him all about her bravery under the attacks she had endured and survived.   But in her present situation she couldn't allow her ears to hear herself confess to her vulnerabilities.   She needed to stand strong in her own eyes.   She needed to prove to Jack and herself she was impenetrable and undaunted in the face of danger.   In so many ways, Caroline found herself reflecting on her sister in law, Crystal who had been through a great deal of life or death situations of her own.   Had it not been for Crystal's innate savvy and expertise with a gun, she, no doubt, would have met with a gruesome demise just as Caroline might have with Don McPoland. The only difference that Caroline could see was that Crystal was truly a tougher, more resilient person than she.

Chapter Four
The dangers of complacency

There was to be no trial or further investigation after the case came to a close.   At no time did any evidence come forward that would give the detectives any reason to further investigate the case of the East Coast Strangler.   With a sigh of relief, Caroline was told that her services would no longer be needed as far as any more questioning or deposition.   The case was closed.   And to Caroline's relief, her identity was never exposed. As if she was enrolled in the services of the Witness Protection Program, the police department respected Caroline's wishes to remain completely anonymous. All the while, her name and face stayed out of the papers, she felt, however, it was just a matter of time before somebody or something would slip up and reveal her identity.   But until that day, she continued to live cautiously and thankful for not having to take to the road again, on the run.   Quite frankly, she was enjoying her new job with the real estate business, and she was quite proud of her progress, surpassing the income she had working for the film company by three fold.   Everything seemed to be falling into place rather nicely, save the absence of the love of her life.   After the sixth month of living in the upper class element and the comfort of security, Caroline feared only one thing; her complacency.   Should she become slack in her responsibility to keep steady vigil, the unfortunate consequences could prove to be fatal.   Every week, when business might have been slowed, Caroline took the time to keep up with her accuracy skills out at the shooting range.   Though she understood that ninety-nine point nine percent of the time her attacker will be within inches and not yards from her, she still wanted to be readily familiar with her sidearm.   She had also taken a few extra precautions when driving around her neighborhood, looking for escape routs should she be followed or chased.   As a precaution, she bought an old junky Buick that dated back to the late seventies.   She had the machine overhauled and tuned to it's newest specifications.   After buying a new set of tires for it and a spare, she filled the trunk with non-perishable foods, blankets, clothes, wigs and cash.   She put the Buick in a twenty-four hour storage facility.   Should the unfortunate time arise, the spare car would be available and always at her disposal.   The car was strategically parked at the back of the lot where the front end was facing a chin link fence.   Hoping the time would never occur, Caroline was always ready to use the car at any given time.   With a heavy duty chain and pad lock in the trunk of her Jaguar, she was ready to lead her followers to the gate of the storage facility.   If timed correctly, she would be able to lock the gate behind her and then with the use of bolt-cutters, she also had in the trunk, she would be able to drive through the chain link fence into the parking lot of the opposite building.   She mocked trialed the effort several times making sure she was able to accomplish her task in under two minutes. Seemingly, all precautions had been exercised and that's what was bothering Caroline.   A nagging worry kept at her subconscious leading her to believe she had missed something.   Perhaps her worrisome thoughts were nothing more than a maternal habit keeping her on her toes and fully alert, but the fact remained in her gut, she wasn't doing enough to protect her daughter and their identity.   Month after month, Carline studied all possible ramifications, should Little Chief and his posse find them.   To no avail could she pacify her mind enough to keep from worrying.   The incessant feelings of danger would continually inhibit her ability to think clearly. Though it was an isolated case, having been attacked by Don McPoland, she couldn't help but think how easily he could have been an affiliated L.A. gang member attempting to retaliate for the death of Big Mike.   Even Jack was having trouble getting any dependable intel on this particular gang, which didn't help ease her mind.

Perhaps it was a mother's instinctive nature, or maybe a psychic premonition, either way, it first happened when Caroline was in bed for the night, only six months since the day she and El settled in West Palm Beach.   Her mind was adrift, just before sleep.   It was that period of limbo when the mind is attentively bridging the connections between the subconscious and the waking consciousness.   All at once, Caroline shot up in bed, frightened and mystified by her vision.   Though her thoughts were somewhat distorted and viewed through a foggy haze, the basis of the premonition was clear enough to be understood by her.   There was no doubt what she was feeling or seeing as it unfolded in her mind in less than a second, was that of imminent danger. The helpless feeling of being outnumbered was her immediate fright.   The great number of opposition was what caught her off guard and feeling instantly overwhelmed and helplessly defeated.   Each enemy with firearms of automatic firing capability was what came to mind as the vision would unfold.   Clearly, the vision was a warning, but the evidence was yet to unfold.   A time or a place of such an attack was never detected.   Her mind was whirring with fears of her having fallen into a contented false sense of security.   If only she could have understood the exact meaning of the vision, she might have been able to understand her role to protect her child, but instead, the vision made her feel uneasy and inadequate with all that she had done until now. Only after several hours was she able to calm herself enough to sleep through the night. The very next morning, however, the feeling of imminent danger was equally evident. She couldn't manage the uneasy feeling that crept under her skin. So many times, she wanted to call Jack to find out what information he had found on Little Chief, but her righteous pride kept her from making that call. She already knew that if he had something important to share with her, he would have already called. Though her heart told her to pack up and run, she chose to stay and see what might unfold. Her logic played a bigger role in her decision making. One of her biggest fears was that she might have been putting too much faith in Jacks ability to keep them protected.

Chapter Five
The Break in

	The address of the hit was scrolled across a yellow legal pad two of the boys had sitting on the seat between them. Inundated with several empty cans of soda, bags of pretzels and several Hero Sub sandwich wrappers, the car might have served better as a trash can. But their drive had been long and the orders were to be executed immediately. Inside information had revealed that police evidence was reported to be relocated soon. Subsequently, the boss wasn't wasting any time with this one. It was a job only two soldiers were contracted to. Two would be more than enough. On the pad, the address read 239 Wisconsin Ave, Huron, South Dakota. The boys had traveled across several states to make this hit. And this hit served as a very important right of passage for the new recruits. Anytime new recruits might get an important mission handed down by the boss personally shows one of two very important things; either the boss is impressed with his new soldiers, or he feels they are expendable should they fail, or even succeed, depending on the boss's needs. In any event, this was a golden opportunity to prove themselves worthy of higher rank in the echelon of authority within the ranks of the hierarchy. The syndicate works on a value system that places high value on jobs well done and merit performances. Oddly, the younger recruits were willing to do much of anything to gain the respect that they craved from the upper ranking members. The more dangerous the job to be performed, the better the feeling they might gain after accomplishing the task requested of them. In this case, the job was relatively easy, but the task was very important to the boss. To fail the job and be caught by the police or other authority was nothing in comparison to what the boss would do to the boys. It was a do or die position that they volunteered for gleefully. An opportunity like this one didn't come often. The instructions were simple, and the location of interest was in plain site, but the recourses of execution would be left up to the boys once they got to their destination.

In less than fifteen hours of travel, the boys found the mark. After inspecting the neighborhood and checking out all the immediate resources, the boys worked out a viable plan most suitable for a successful heist. However, this wasn't just any heist. It wasn't about making a big score on money, nor was it about taking out a witness. It was a quest for information necessary to follow through on a vendetta…a long over due vendetta. It was only a few hours until nightfall. According to the posted hours on the glass doors of the building, the employees, would be emptying out around 5:00 PM. As they talked between themselves they came up with a clever plan that would aid in their success. First, they filled up the tank of their car. Knowing that once the crime would be commenced, there would be no time to make any stops while fleeing. Once the plan went into effect, they knew they only had a few short minutes to getaway from the crime scene and make their way back to California where their headquarters were. After filling the tank of their car, they studied the neighborhood of the building in question. The Municipal building of the South Dakota Police Department was their target and query. The front glass door of the building was far too narrow to plow their way through, but upon further inspection, they found that the back doors were plenty wide to effect a viable break in. The next plan was to find a vehicle they could steal and use as the battering ram for their entry into the building.   To their surprise, they noticed a tire store right next door to the Police Department.   Taking into account that every second would be valuable time lost should they have to travel from one place to another, having a tire shop right next door couldn't have been more perfect.   And to the their good fortune, the tire shop would close at 5:00 PM sharp as well.   The homework of their deed was simple. They located the work truck to the tire store behind the building.   The store kept the truck overnight from within a locked chain link fence.   Evidently, no cameras were anywhere in sight.   And the truck was dated from the mid eighties.   Jacking that particular model truck would pose no challenge to the well practiced duo.   Knowing that they already had a set of bolt cutters in the trunk of their car, the plan seemed to be an easy task.

While waiting for the sun to set and the streets to become quiet, the two boys set out to complete the planning of the job.   The bolt cutters were hidden under the jacket of the bigger boy while the other loaded and checked the pistols.   Between the two of them, they had four hand guns and nearly twenty fully loaded magazines.   Making sure they wouldn't have trouble reloading if the need should arise, they used nine mm hand guns only.   Though they might not have had a lot of training in the field with guns, they certainly had a great deal of training with stealing cars and breaking into buildings.   The syndicate of their origin took pride in showing their soldiers the most effective way of winning battles. And knowing that efficiency was one way of enforcing a winning edge against the enemy, the boys stuck to the plan they had practiced to this point.

At 7:15, the boys parked their car around the back alley of the adjacent tire shop.   If in case there were hidden cameras, they would be clear of them once the action took place.   With ski masks on their faces and all the hardware necessary for a war, the boys set out to work.   On foot, they ambled on over to the tire store.   Once they saw the path was clear of any obstacles or witnesses at the tire store, they used the bolt cutters to cut the pad lock on the gate. They quietly and quickly opened the gate, propping it open for their escape.   The truck wasn't locked, but the keys were no where in sight.   But it didn't matter to them.   Just as they had suspected, the ignition was easy to hotwire.   Once the truck was started, they went to work driving the truck out of the parking area of the tire store and directly across the street to the Police Department.   Using the back ally to the back of the building, the driver approached the back doors cautiously looking to see if any one was around.   Once they were certain that the place was quiet and there were no witnesses, the driver moved deftly to turn the rear of the truck to face the doors. After throwing the truck in reverse, he stepped on the gas with a squeal to the tires.   The crashing impact tossed the truck around like it were a toy.   However, the truck had served it's purpose.   The driver put the truck in drive and pulled it out of the way.   The double doors of the building was obliterated giving open unhindered passage.   Leaving the truck running, the two boys jumped out of the truck with the doors left open and entered the building with flashlights already in one hand and their pistols in the other.   Their agenda was simple, though the task of finding the evidence room proved to be the only hindrance they would encounter.   Only one of the boys knew how to read sufficiently.   As one would shine the light at the title-sign of each room, the other would keep a look out, poised and ready to defend. At one point while the two were trying to find the right room, they hadn't noticed the night watchman silently walking up on them.   He was a skilled police officer trained to serve and protect the public. But what he didn't expect was the response he got from the two hoodlums bent on steeling evidence from the evidence room.   The very moment the two boys noticed the cop had the advantage on them, a sudden and explosive hail of gunfire took place. There was no reasoning or plea bargain to use for an amicable resolve.   There wasn't even a second to speak out a deal.   Though the officer was wearing a Kevlar vest, he took gunfire, instantly knocking him off his feet.   The smaller of the two boys who couldn't have been more than fifteen was the next to be hit by gunfire.   The .45 caliber bullet used by the police officer nearly cut the boy in half, the cop fired repeatedly in self defense.   As the shots rang out, another individual came from the front of the building to aid the officer.   Apparently he too was a cop, only a plain clothed cop.   With his gun drawn and firing as well, the barrage of   bullets rang out with a deafening report.   Muzzle blasts and gunfire was all anyone could hear or see for several seconds. The younger boy who took the first bullet was the first to die in a puddle of his own blood on the floor of the administration building.   Using his body as a shield, the larger of the two boys managed to disable the officer after firing several rounds into the unprotected parts of his body.   Magazine after magazine, the boy kept firing and exchanging guns assuring his mission would succeed.   The plain clothed cop held his ground, though unable to aid his bleeding comrade, he wouldn't quit or relent.   With every attempt to reach for the downed officer, the boy would impede his will by firing several rounds. Both cops were armed with Glock 17s using .45 caliber bullets, however, neither one of them were equipped with the number of magazines that the boys came armed with.   As the cop made every attempt to use his ammo frugally and effectively, the boy would answer with hail of return.   And before the second cop got the chance to call for backup, he took a ricochet bullet to the leg.   To his misfortune, the wound sliced through his femoral artery causing a substantial loss of blood.   In an attempt to save his life and the life of his fellow officer he had to withdraw his offensive pose and pull back to safety.

Soon after the boy realized the battle had come to an end, he quickly responded by continuing with his search.   As he carefully snaked his way around the building, he kept vigil for the wounded officer.   Only one office looked to be lighted as the rest of the building was dark and eerily quiet.

Then, the sudden dialogue opened up with the officer inquiring as to what the boy needed.   "What ever it is you are looking for, I'm sure it's not worth throwing your life away over, son.   You could save yourself a lot of grief if you would let me help my partner."   The sound of shuffling with the squeal of door opening was the only answer the officer would hear.   "Come on son, it doesn't need to be like this. You can take whatever it is you came for, and you could be doing us a big favor by letting me get help for my friend.   Unfortunately, the officer was too far from his cell phone that was left on his desk, and there were no land lines in the records room he took refuge in.

"I ain't helping nobody.   You just tell me where the evidence room is and I might let you two fools live."   The boy was adamant as he was heartless.   He had only one goal in mind, and that was to make his boss proud.

"That's the easy part, young man.   The evidence room is downstairs in the basement, but you will need my keys to get through the door.   All this bloodshed could have been avoided if only you had asked first."   His attempt at reasoning fell on deaf ears as the reply came without remorse or consideration.

"Throw the keys out of the room, or there *will* be a lot more bloodshed, pig."

Knowing the boy was obviously after something from the evidence room.   He could only hope that he would leave the building once he retrieved it.   "Here, take them…"   Officer Mallory tossed the keys through the doorway and out into the hall of where he was taking shelter behind a filing cabinet.   "It's the big silver one marked 1127 on it."

Though the assailant said nothing, Officer Mallory heard the keys being lifted off the tiled floor of the hallway.   The boy, then, proceeded to head down the stairs as his footsteps gave hint to his whereabouts.

Officer Mallory hesitated to say anything further.   As much as he wanted to bargain for his life and the life of his fellow officer, it was clear to him that there was no bargaining chip to work with. The kid was malicious and had no compassion for life.   The officer chose to remain quiet and take cover should the boy return.   His only advantage was the fact that the records room was very dark, and the boy would have no idea of the layout should he decide to enter and finish off the officer.

The clinging of keys was followed by the sound of the basement door opening.   Then there was nothing but silence.   In less than five minutes, the boy was making his way back up the steps to the main hallway.   Without saying another word, the kid exited the building.   The only way that the officer knew that he had left the building was hearing the engine of the truck being revved as the kid squealed the tires and accelerated out of the back alleyway.   Though officer Mallory had used his shirt as a tourniquet in the attempt to stop the bleeding, he had suffered a great loss of blood .   Without wasting another second, the officer crawled to the adjacent office to find the closest land line.   Within seconds, he dialed and spoke with the 911 operator.   It took nearly three minutes for the ambulance and half the local police force to arrive.   Fortunately, officer Mallory survived the incursion.   However, officer Manson bleed out and died long before help had arrived.

The young boy with a bullet wound to his shoulder and another to his calf muscle managed to race the truck back to his car without being seen or detected by anyone.   He slipped out of town in his own car before the cops had dispatched a search party.   Though an All Points Bulletin (APB) had been announced on all the police radios, somehow the young boy managed to elude the cops and make his way back to California.   No doubt, his boss must have been proud.

Chapter Six
Gang Relations

The boy made his trek all the way back to California without being detected or bleeding out. As soon as he handed the file box marked Hammora case to the boss, young Topper's wounds were treaded by the house doctor.   Topper's wounds turned out too be superficial and not life-threatening.

The boss, who went by the simple name of Trey was very pleased with his soldiers dedication to the family's cause.   Living as a gang member, throughout most of his life, Trey was the leader of what he called his family of soldiers.   He promised young Topper that good deeds done in respect to the welfare and profit of the family would always be rewarded with rank and monetary gain.   "Money is the way of the world, Baby"   Trey would always say as his mantra.   Though Trey was supposedly a spiritual man who believed in meditation and in the ways of nurturing the mind, he seemed to have a distorted way of looking at the facts at hand.   He always believed that he should be the one to grab the cookie from the cookie jar so that no one else could. A sort of survival of the fittest law applied to the concrete village of Los Angeles as well as in the jungle of life in general.

His story begins with him being raised by his mother and step dad.   His true father died as a soldier in a gang.   Both his mother and two brothers believed his father to be an outstanding hero.   He lived to be thirty-nine, and made his family a very profitable income and a fierce reputation.   He lived far longer than any other in his line of work.   His lessons in fighting and gorilla warfare were still in effect long after his death.   And everything he knew to be strong and right with people and family, he taught to his oldest son, Trey.   Long after the shooting death of his father, Trey practiced the teachings of his father to his two brothers and to all of his top soldiers.   His way of life was bred into his business and dealing with others.   His philosophy was undeniably effective with his soldiers.   He taught lessons in humility and lessons in survival. His mainstay was his father and from the day of his death to present, he took over the roll of mentor and boss.   And though Trey was a very big man in both size and reputation, his persona was a demand for respect and obedience.   As an example of a typical day as a juvenile, Trey was asked by his little brother Mike to pick up a friend at his place of work.   Mike was yet too young to be driving on his own, so Trey was only to happy and proud to take his little brother for a ride.   Mike's friend named Tom was about the same age as he, around fifteen or so.   Tom worked for his father at the local liquor store every day after school.   On this particular day, Tom was allowed to take off from work early inasmuch as his dad had personal business to take care of and didn't want his son within earshot while the deal was going down. Unbeknown to Mike until the moment they arrived at the liquor store was an old adversary dating back to grade school when Mike would get beat up by this big bully named Jimmy.   Right away, just as Trey pulled the car up into the parking lot of the liquor store and kills the engine, Mike sighs a deep breath, knowing that Jimmy would be causing trouble as he always did.   Jimmy was a big boy.   He was always the tallest in the class and the strongest.   At the age of ten, he had already reached the height of five foot, five inches.   At the age of fifteen, he was six foot, two inches and weighing in at a hundred and ninety pounds of nothing but lean angriness.   Nobody ever understood why the guy was always so angry and quick to pick a fight with Mike, but everyone knew if the two were seen together, it no doubt, would result in an ugly brawl, usually with Mike losing miserably.

As Mike stepped out of his brother's car, he had a horrible feeling that Jimmy would be starting trouble for him.   It was obvious that Jimmy saw and recognized him the moment Mike and his brother pulled up.   Jimmy with his bottle of beer in hand, sitting on the hand rail of the wheelchair ramp leading into the liquor store, opened his big mouth just as Mike had suspected.   Before Jimmy even opened his mouth, Mike could just feel the bitter rancor coming off the guy.

"Hey, faggot, what brings you here?" Jimmy barked with his habitual rancor. Though Jimmy was only fifteen years of age and much too young to be drinking alcohol, Tom's dad would always sell him beer lest he might break the windows of the storefront as he had done before.

Mike stepped out of the car hopping his brother Trey didn't hear what Jimmy had said.   "It's best you don't say anything around my brother, Jimmy.   He's got a real bad temper, and you don't want any of that."   Mike said as he walked up toward the ramp, trying to pacify the situation by being calm and collected.

Unfortunately, Jimmy didn't see things quite the way Mike had intended.   "What's that you say, faggot, you brought your girlfriend along?"   Jimmy laughed with a mocking tone and with a cocky disposition, pointing his finger at Trey with the beer nearly spilling from the same hand.

A loud bellow of a reverberating voice suddenly emitted from the car.   "WHAT THE FUCK?"   Trey had the unbelievable ability to pull his bass voice from the bowels of his inner soul deeply seeded somewhere between Hell and the Devil's private lair.

Quite suddenly, Mike felt his heart lodge up into his throat. "Oh, man, you shouldn't have said that." Mike announced, fearing the worst. Already hearing the squeak of the door as his brother exited the car, Mike knew what was to happen next. He didn't need to turn and look, the inevitable was already occurring. Trey was already out of the car and slowly making his appearance from around the other side. Even with Trey's enormous stature and obvious brawn, Jimmy kept on blabbing his mouth of insipid obscenities and fearless bragging.

"No, it's okay bro, you don't need to come kiss me. I don't do faggots." Still laughing, Jimmy never once realized what dangers he was toying with until it was, far, too late for a merciful reprieve.

As Trey made his way up the ramp, Mike whispered in Jimmy's ear, "I told you to shut the fuck up, but you were too stupid to see death coming. This is your fault, fool. You should have listened." Mike had no intention of pitting his brother against Jimmy, but once the Dawg is out of the kennel there's no putting him back. "Just remember, Jimmy, the pain you are about to suffer now isn't one tenth of what you've been dishin' out…" Mike made his way up the ramp, but before he opened the door to go inside the liquor store, he hesitated. It had been a long time since he had seen his brother go to work. In a fleeting moment, Mike decided to stay outside and watch the fireworks.

With Trey working up a fury that a blind person would have been able to see, Jimmy never once suspected the ominous nightmare that was coming his way. All his life, Jimmy had picked on

the weak and the disabled, snatching purses from
older ladies and beating on people half his size.
Now, it was time for him to meet his match.

Trey would generally be a calm sort of guy.
Much of the time, most wouldn't see his true anger
until he was already half way into a fight.   One time,
Trey was seen by his brother Mike punching himself
in the face seconds before a fight just to get himself
mad enough to fight effectively.   He had a
philosophy that was quite opposite of most; using his
anger and adrenalin to promote a higher level of
power was more to his penchant.   But this time was
different.   Trey was already mad-dog angry because
somebody was picking on his family, and that
somebody had gotten him to the highest level of fury
Mike had ever seen.   Jimmy's ignorance, no doubt,
sparked the greater and shortest of Trey's fuse.
From that moment of ignition, there was no turning
back.   As Trey stood nose to nose with Jimmy, a
crowed began to gather from those within the store
and those who might have been passing by.   Being
the tyrant of the neighborhood, there were quite a few
people who wouldn't have minded seeing Jimmy get
his ass kicked for a change.   Both gladiator looking
men, clad in white wife beaters and dark pants looked
even in height.   Though Jimmy was lean and well
defined muscularly, Trey was a tank with very little
definition, but a lot of width.   His physique was the
epitome of massive power and overwhelming
strength.   Breaking the silence with a thunderous
roar, Trey opened up with a dialogue only Mike
would have expected.   "You're obviously too
ignorant or drunk to understand the pounding you are
about to receive, so consider yourself lucky if I don't
happen to feel like ripping off your head and shitting
down your neck.   Or maybe, I should fuck you in
the ass since I'm a faggot.   Don't you find me real

pretty, boy?"   With lightning speed, Trey grabbed hold of Jimmy's hand with the beer bottle still in his clutch.

Seeming only a little less confident, Jimmy made the mistake of not backing down when he might have had the chance.   And instead, he made a second mistake of opening his mouth once again.   "Damn, you really are a flamin' faggot.   And let go of my hand.   I don't want no part of you, fucker."   Jimmy struggled to get his hand free, but his efforts were hopelessly futile.

"Now, I asked you a question.   I expect the respect of an answer from you.   Tell me how pretty you think I am and you might survive the day."   Calmly, Trey said, applying more muscle to his grip around Jimmy's hand.

More people joined the crowd that came to investigate the ruckus.

"Hey, fuck you, asshole."   Jimmy bellowed.   With little thought, Jimmy struck a closed fisted blow to the side of Trey's jaw.

Trey didn't budge.   He stood rock-solid like a brass statue.   Exponentially, Trey applied more and more squeeze to his deadly grip at Jimmy's hand that was now feeling the pressure of a vise-grip.   "I'll let that go for now, princess.   But I'm still waiting for an answer from you."   Trey's seriousness was not to be mistaken.   His bounty of steadfast power was no match for Jimmy's cowardice repertoire.

"What the hell's wrong with you, Dawg…you're hurting my hand."   Jimmy was finally getting the point of his lesson of the day.   The look in his face was quickly turning from confidence to a hesitant school boy.   Mike could virtually see the dilemma stirring in Jimmy's mind, trying to decide whether to hit the opposition, once again, or give into Trey's game of mind tricks.

"I'm not going to ask you again, princess. Give me an answer, or you will die right here on this spot, bloodied and fucked in the ass so hard, I believe you will fall in love with me before you take your last breath."   Trey was not fooling around.   Anyone could see the veins in his neck and shoulders were growing with a pulsing beat by the second.

"FUCK YOU!"   Shouted Jimmy, trying to remain calm in the company of   Mr. death himself. His fear was written all over his face, as he tried to look tough in the eyes of the growing crowd.

Calmly, Trey looked deeply in Jimmy's eyes. "Wrong answer."   Replied Trey, taking a deep breath a second before he made his next move. With the summoned power of his fury and despise for such ignorance, Trey exploded a warrant for an over-supply of adrenalin to rush directly to his hand.   In an instant, the beer bottle shattered sounding like a popping balloon from within Jimmy's hand. Instantly, the mix of foaming beer and the crimson liquid of Jimmy's blood-letting was spilling uninhibited on the concrete ramp of the liquor store. Jimmy looked to be in shock as Trey kept his grip over him showing no signs of relent or weakness.   It wasn't until that moment, of shattered glass and sudden pain, that Jimmy realized he had messed with the wrong guy.

"I'm still waiting."   Trey kept his vise-grip firmly wrapped around Jimmy's bleeding hand.

"Okay, yeah, you're a real pretty dude. Now, let me go."   Jimmy was feverishly wriggling as best he could to remove Trey's stronghold.   Even with the aid of his other hand, Jimmy was ineffective at freeing himself.

The hush of the phalanges crowd who had been watching the entire time, became emphatic and louder, showing their support for the breaking of the town bully.

Mike stepped up to Jimmy offering his advise, "I told you to shut the fuck up, but you just had to mouth off to my brother Trey…"

"Trey? Trey Rollins is your brother? You are Trey Rollins?" Jimmy was in tears by now as the pool of blood grew larger as it would stream down the ramp, smelling of beer. "I didn't know. I'm sorry. I was just foolin' around." The tears of pain were already streaming down both Jimmy's cheeks.

"No, it's too late, dude. I tried to warn you." Mike said, beginning to enjoy the suffering he was witnessing. After years of badgering and endless suffering at the hands of a cowardice bully, it was time for Mike to make the demands now.

"Whatever you need, I can get it for you…ahhh." Jimmy cried out in pain as Trey began to grind the shards of class in his shifting, squeezing grip.

"You have nothing anyone in this town wants, Jimmy. In fact, nobody here wants *you* in this town." Mike was only too happy to be conveying the same interest of the people.

"Amen to that." Chimed, Mr. Washington, the owner of the liquor store, peeking his head out from the front door.

"Anyone here have any use for this guy?" Mike asked, turning and addressing the people who had gathered around and seemed to be taking pleasure in seeing Jimmy finally get a bit of his own medicine. After seeing there wasn't one positive response from anyone, Mike looked to Jimmy with a resolute look on his face. "Well, there ya have it, Jimmy; no one seems to like having you around. He's all yours, bro." Mike said, showing no remorse whatsoever.

Trey had Jimmy on his knees in fear for his life.   The painful shards of glass had impaled deeper into his hand as Trey's grip continued to grind and knead relentlessly.   "I will tell you what…I'm not in the mood to kill anyone today.   How about you, little brother, you in the mood?"

"Not really,   I had plans for tonight.   And these are my school clothes, and you know how mad Mom gets when she finds blood on my school clothes."   Mike seemed to appreciate the laughter he got from some the crowd.

"Then it's settled.   Trey announced.   "After you wake, up you will get the hell out of this neighborhood.   And if any of these kind folks around here tell me they have seen you around, I promise I will find you, and I will kill you, and leave your dead ass to rot in the street.   You feel me, fool?"

As soon as Jimmy shook his head in agreement, Trey punched Jimmy in the face knocking him out cold.   By the time the encounter was finally all over, Jimmy had lost at least a pint of blood.   But the good news was, after Jimmy came to, he was never seen again.

From that day on, Mike had gained the new handle of Big Mike.   It was never clear as to why Mike got the accolades for Trey's work, nevertheless, that's how it all happened.   The notorious LA gang was feared, respected and praised, from that day on, for protecting the neighborhood from short-minded hoodlums like Jimmy Whitefield.

Chapter Seven
The Investigation

Trey spent hours poring over the contents of the box that Topper had procured for him.   The police report had little information on the woman who had entered the mini-mart on the day the clerk of that store was murdered.   The only witness to the robbery and resulting murder had simply slipped through the cracks of every jurisdiction and possible discovery to her identity.   The only possibility of finding out who the woman might be was evidence found on a video tape.   The mini-mart had their own surveillance tape that was collected by the South Dakota Police Department after the robbery and brutal murder of the retail clerk.   Inasmuch as she and her little girl were never found pertinent to the case. The police never investigated her identity.

It was Big Mike's misfortune to have lost his life that same fateful day.   He and his crew were on a country wide trek to gather funds from clients for recent drug transactions.   Big Mike's territory covered the entire mid-west region.

What bothered Trey the most was his inability to find any evidence anywhere leading to who killed his little brother.   His hunch was keen, thinking that the woman from the video tape may have had something to do with the loss of his entire crew,   but nothing was adding up to a substantial lead.   Even the house where Big Mike's body was found along with his crew left no lead for Trey to search.   As his anger grew exponentially with every failed inquiry, Trey vowed unconditionally to avenge his brother's death.   Even if it meant breaking into the evidence room of every police department across the entire country, he swore to make good on his promise.

        Al Rollins, known as Little Chief was the diplomat of the family.   He preferred diplomacy over force, and peaceful treaties in lieu of cold murder.   His attribute to the business end of the family was his ability to attain substantial financial gain.   He dealt in guns, drugs and prostitution. Always dressed in a nice suit, Little Chief handled business his way, amicably and with a certain finesse that generally got the same results as his older and younger brother, he had a penchant for running guns as it was a profitable business. There wasn't a firearm made that he didn't know about.   His own personal arsenal was a collection of fine work.   From his pair of gold plated Colt 1911's to his custom made AK-47's, he had taken pride and a great deal of time collecting the various kinds of guns that pleased him best.   And though he wasn't an NRA member, Little Chief once bid on and won a very special gun at a very prestigious auction.   The gun was previously owned by Charleston Heston, the president of the NRA, until his illness in 2003 which precluded him from continuing on.   Little Chief's own private collection also included a replica of the Peacemaker that Wyatt Earp carried during his time served as a Peace Officer.   Many of the family members believed that Little Chief must have been a gunslinger of the Western days in a past life.   While most of his posse were carrying automatic, magazine loading hand guns, Little Chief kept to his revolver, claiming it was a far more dependable gun.
        Little Chief took to the streets soon after he

found the fate of his little brother, Big Mike.   His mission was to find any information on who was responsible for his death.   Both Trey and Little chief took their brother's death very hard.   No amount of passivity would allow Big Mike's death to go unanswered.   As far as diplomacy was concerned, Little Chief only believed in one thing and that was, "an eye for an eye".

Chapter Eight
Comfort in being on the road

El's seventh birthday was coming up.   The incessant nagging from El to see her daddy was overwhelming for Caroline, to say the least. Perhaps it was the child's innate ability to perceive just how close she was to convincing her mother to give in to her pleas.

Finally, after much thought and convincing persuasion, just a couple of weeks before her birthday, Caroline, indeed, gave in.   She herself, couldn't stand to be without her family for such a long period of time.   She figured, a week long visit couldn't hurt too terribly.   Caroline had given word to Jack that she would be driving in.   She chose not to fly inasmuch as she was unable to carry any weapons on the flight.   And besides, Caroline had grown an affinity to driving long distances.   Not only did she feel more secure while on the road, but she enjoyed the private time with her daughter.   As the days to travel back to the West coast grew closer, Caroline had made all the arrangements with her boss, Fred, and she had also arranged for a rental van. Knowing the Jaguar would be too uncomfortable for such a long drive, she picked out a luxurious van to use for the trip.   The same place that rents motor-homes to travelers, also provides vans and trucks of various sizes and shapes.   The van she picked out came equipped with a fancy little kitchen with a sink and a one burner stove.   Though it didn't have a restroom, it was rather accommodating just the same. The far back seats folded to a very large bed, and so did the middle row of seats.   In addition, there was plenty of storage space for luggage and food supplies. By packing a large ration of food, Caroline wouldn't need to make as many stops along the way except to use the restrooms and fill up for gas.   As Caroline drew out the itinerary for their trip, she made sure to avoid South Dakota entirely.   Using the southern routs, she made every effort to steer clear of any states that might bring up any of her past deeds with gang members.   As the day for travel grew closer, the two of them became excited with the prospect of seeing the family.   Feeding on each other's excitement made the whole preparation that much more fun for them.   In the back of her mind, Caroline pondered that she was probably doing the wrong thing by giving in so easily, but she had already warned El and Jack that it would only be a week's visit.   Of course, El seemed to believe differently.   She knew, only too well, how much Mommy loved Daddy.   She wasn't always asleep when she would hear Mommy up late at night crying over Daddy.

With the map of the United States unfolded across the kitchen table, El   studied the rout that her mom was considering.   Immediately she recognized the state of South Dakota, claiming that Cookie Monster had taken a bite out of the top right-hand corner of the state, and that the bottom right-hand corner had melted into Nebraska.   At least, that was how her teacher taught the kids to learn where they lived.   When El turned her attention to the state of Florida she immediately found the city of West Palm Beach.   Proving her daddy right as his prodigy, El enquired about the Northern compass at the lower part of the map.   "Which way is East and West again, Mommy?"

Caroline took her marker and wrote in the W, the E and the S for South.   "That's what it should look like, sweetie.   I guess the artist assumes everyone knows where they go.

"Thank you, Mommy."   El further studied

the map.   No doubt, she was quite a prodigy -- not yet seven years old, and already finding locations on a map.   "I think you got it backwards, Mommy." El pointed to the East coast of Florida where West Palm Beach clearly showed it's location in big bold letters.   And on the opposite of Florida's peninsula was where El pointed out what must have been the West coast.   "See Mommy, we live over here on the west, so this must be the East."   El then pointed to the other side.   Her logic made perfect sense.

Caroline had never before thought about the oddity of the map.   "I guess we are both right. Boy, you really are smart.   Perhaps you should right the Chamber of Commerce a letter and have them change the name of our city to East Palm Beach. Because, clearly, you are right; we should be living over here on the West side of the state."

"I'm not a boy, Mommy."   Sternly, El looked at her mother making pensive eyebrows.   "It was probably a stupid boy who made the mistake on the map.   Johnny got a D in geography.   Maybe it was his dad that made this map."   Still looking pensive and perplexed, she asked her mom,   "Do you think after writing a letter, the Shamer Conference will fix the name of our city?"

"I doubt it, baby.   Because then everyone in the city would have to change their address on all their envelopes.   And that would be a lot of work."

El puckered her lips in deep thought.   "Then I don't want to write a letter."   El folded her arms in protest.   "The boss of the city is just going to ignore my letter anyways."

Caroline looked directly at her brilliant daughter.   "You're probably right, sweetie, welcome to the real world."

On the first day of the trip, Caroline brought

the van home from the rental place.   She had nearly
packed the entire vehicle by the time El got home
from school.   Just seeing the van in the driveway
gave little El a chill of excitement as she screamed
with joy, running into the house immediately after the
buss dropped her off.   El grabbed her mom, hugging
her tight and longingly.   No words were needed,
they both knew how happy the occasion was.   Soon
after shedding her school clothes, El finished her last
minute packing and loaded her own suitcase into the
van.   The van was so large and roomy inside, El
assumed that Mom hadn't yet packed it.   To her
surprise, El's last minute things were the only items
left to be packed.

        Having taken the day off, Caroline had plenty
of time to arrange and hide her arsenal of weaponry
within the little hidden spaces and compartments of
the van.   Even a few wigs were packed along with
the luggage.   Caroline had changed her appearance
so many times along the way to the East coast, she
was beginning to worry if she might forget what she
had looked like last in each state.   Figuring that she
could never be too careful, she brought all her wigs
for safety sake.

        The timing seemed to have worked out well,
appropriately so, the gas water heater had stopped
working properly the night before.   Each time
Caroline would attempt to light the pilot light, the
flame would extinguish itself immediately after she
would release the valve button.   Knowing they
would be out of town for a couple of weeks, she
made a call to the landlord giving him plenty of time
to fix the problem.   The only unfortunate timing was
the making of a chilling shower Caroline was forced
to take that morning.   And the more she thought
about Jack and what greetings he may have planned
for her, the colder the damned water became as the

last of the heated water had supplied itself out completely.

After a last minute scan through the checklist, Caroline made her way through the house checking that all the doors and windows were locked and secured.   The moment of departure had arrived.   It had been well over a year since either of them had seen Jack or the family.   The chill of excitement and anticipation struck them both as they shut and locked the front door of the house.   They decided the first stop would be to pick up some fast food.   Caroline had already filled the gas tank before she brought the van to the house.   As they climbed into the van and buckled up, they looked at each other with a glee they hadn't felt for some time.

Caroline turned the key to the ignition.   The roar of the big engine came to life giving a chilling thrill to the both of them.   The long, anticipated trip across the country back home was finally at hand. As promised, they stopped off at the drive through of a McDonalds for a quick bite.   Caroline ordered a chicken sandwich, and El ordered her regular chicken nugget box with honey mustard dip.   And as always, the inevitable questions of a young mind would arise without fail.

"Mommy, what part of the chicken is this?" El held up a half eaten chicken nugget with a tiny crescent shape added to it.

"They claim it's the white meat, so I'm assuming it's the breast."   Said Mom, already detecting the line of questioning welling up in Little El's face.

"Mommy, you're just being silly.   Chickens don't have boobies."   Little El said, actually believing her mom had made a funny.

After Caroline had good laugh, she explained the difference between the chicken breast and the female anatomy.   However, even after explaining it to her daughter, the explanation seemed a bit odd to the both of them.

"I think they should have called it chicken chests.   I think Mr. Mc Donald has too much sex on his mind."

And after another good, hearty laugh, Caroline proudly said, "And there you have it, the mind of an analytical thinker; destined to be the next philosopher, attorney or even the next president."

"I don't know what a fossfutter is, but it doesn't sound like fun.   I want to be a dolphin trainer."   El announced, no doubt reflecting on her trip to Marineland where El and Caroline got adventurous and enjoyed an entire day experiencing the many attractions including the Dolphin Encounter.

Caroline was slightly surprised to hear her daughter state such a focused plan for her future, especially considering how El hadn't really enjoyed the encounter at all.   Aside from standing on a platform to pose for the photographer with an actual dolphin for twenty minutes, El was disappointed to find that she wasn't actually allowed to swim with the dolphins as the sales brochure seemed to reflect. Destined to be a lawyer, El pointed out just how unfair the brochure actually was showing the two kids swimming underwater with a real dolphin.

After taking another bite from her breaded chicken McNugget with a heavy dousing of honey mustard dribbling over her fingers, El asked,   "And where do the chickens come from?"   Asked El inquisitively.

"They come from their egg."   Mom answered, knowing more learning adventures would soon follow.

"No, Mommy.   I mean where does the *egg*

come from…cuz Johnny at school said that chickens poop eggs out of their butt, and that's really gross." El grimaced.

"It would seem to me that poor Johnny's ignorance is talking out of a similar orifice."

"Mommy, you know I don't understand what you just said."   El prattled her cute little retort.

"And that would be the point, my genius child.   Mommy needs to stay one step ahead of you at each turn just to make sure you are on your toes, and not heading for any danger.   That's a mommy's job."   Caroline explained hoping to draw her daughter's attention away from the original question.

"Yeah, but where does the egg come from?" El's persistence wasn't detoured   by Mom's sidetracking psychology.

It was at that moment Caroline remembered a joke Jack had told her when they first got together. Jack once told her that he didn't much care to learn which came first; the chicken or the egg.   What he wanted know was which one got *laid* first.   Of course, the joke was far too mature for El's little ears, she did, however look forward to the days when her little girl would be old enough to share such jokes. That being said, Caroline had every intention of keeping her little girl as young and innocent for as long as possible.   No doubt, kids are growing up fast enough.   Trying to be as pragmatic and truthful as possible, Mommy gave her insight of knowledge. "Just like people, chickens have a butt and a front. And the egg, I'm assuming, comes from the front."

"Ouch, doesn't that hurt?"   El's genuine concern was quite cute.

Lord, I hope these questions don't lead to the sex issues of humans.   "I don't know, baby, Mommy doesn't speak chicken."   Desperately attempting to change the subject, Mom asked,   "Did you get enough to eat?   We have lots of fruit and snacks in the back…”

Without skipping a beat, El dove straight into forbidden territory with an onslaught of sensitive questions.   “Johnny says babies come out of mommies stomachs and not their butts…is that true, Mommy.”   El’s intensive stare was demanding answers.

“I think Johnny should keep his pie-hole shut.”   Mommy mumbled under her breath.   “Well, I don’t know anything about where Johnny came from, however, I know for a fact that you came from California, and I was born in California, too.”   Caroline reported, noticing they hadn’t yet traveled the first fifty miles an already, El was trying to grow up too fast.

“I know that part.   Where do babies really come from, Mommy?”

Suddenly feeling a lot like Bill Cosby, or Art Linkletter, before him, Caroline was at a flustering loss for words.   “Well, Johnny was partially right about one thing, the babies do originally come from the mommies stomach.   So when you see a pregnant mommy with her enlarged stomach, you know that that’s where the fetus is growing.”

“So how does the baby come out?”   El asked the million dollar question that Caroline believed was much too young to be told the truth.

It was up to Caroline’s discretion to decide exactly how she would answer that question. “When I was in eighth grade, I attended a health class where the teacher answered all those questions you are asking me now.   I’m afraid you may have to wait until you are in eighth grade before you get the answer to that one, my little princess. Unfortunately, you are much too young to hear the truth.”   Stating the fifth of the constitution of

America, Caroline copped out, hoping to dodge the bullet.

El thought a moment and nonchalantly replied, "The baby probably comes out the front like the egg." Said Little El, taking another bite out of her nugget.

Mom said nothing in reply, as she turned the radio on from the console on the overhead dashboard.

Chapter Nine
Taking care of business

Little Chief had trekked himself across one end of the country to the other ferreting out all possible clues leading him to the person responsible for his brother's death. Checking in only with his brother Trey, the two were impeccably careful not to alert anyone as to their plan to retaliate.   The pact between them was an inseparable bond that no one could deny.   For over six months, Little Chief scoured the countryside, learning nothing other than what Trey was able to provide.   On his cell phone Little Chief reviewed the image of a woman and her young child purchasing ice cream at a mini-mart in a tiny Podunk town in South Dakota.   Trey believed the woman was the only one who could possibly be responsible or might know who was responsible. The only lead was also a dead end.   It wasn't until Trey did some investigating of his own after writing down all the facts pertaining to his brother's death did he decide to pursue another possible lead.   Trey was no slouch working at his computer culling every possible angle of his investigation.   When searching through the police file that Topper had provided, Trey came across the address of where Big Mike had been killed.   Though the police photos showed the residence had been burned to the ground, Trey wasn't discouraged to further his inquiries.   After looking through the Huron County court records on the Assessor's files, he came across the property owner of the house that burned down.   After matching the address with that of the police records, Trey found a perfect match.   Unfortunately, there wasn't a listed phone number for the owner, but that didn't stop Trey.   Furthermore, calling the owner wasn't his true intent anyhow.   In matters of business, Trey always made it a point to meet face to face with clients and opposition alike.

In less than a day after Trey had found a viable clue, Little Chief was already dispatched and making his way to Huron to speak with the property owner.

Chapter Ten
Business As Usual

      The owner of the home that was rented to Caroline and her daughter was a business man who rented a large number of homes and apartments throughout the area.   The house was fully insured and was already at the beginning stages of clean up and reconstruction when Little Chief made his appearance at the job site.   Dressed appropriately fitting as any business man, Little Chief looked and acted the part of a private investigator.   He parked his big, black, shinny Lincoln Town Car at curbside of the construction.   The foreman of the site was the first to greet Little Chief.   Clad in his tool belt and hardhat, the man named Manny introduced himself, looking curiously at the snazzy guy in a expensive trench coat.   Once Little Chief introduced himself and informed the contractor that he was investigating the fire and deaths of the individuals involved in the blaze, Manny seemed more than happy to oblige as best he could.   Though Manny knew nothing of the identities of the people who were caught in the blaze, he was however, able to give out the address and phone number of the owner of the home.   After thanking the man, Little Chief bid him a good day and continued with his investigation.

Just as any private investigator would do, Little Chief followed the lead to a Mr. Hernandez, the owner and landlord of over a dozen rentals in the area.   Without bothering to call the man, Little Chief showed up at Mr. Hernandez's residence that very same day.   Making the meeting and investigation seem as amicable and professional as possible, Little chief conducted business as usual.   He looked over the rental application that Caroline had filled out upon her arrival in town.   After asking the gentleman if he would make a copy of the application, there was little else the man could provide as information was limited.   Being the kind of business man Little Chief was, he opened up his wallet in front of the man and pulled out ten crisp brand new one-hundred dollar bills.   He place each bill on the coffee table, counting out each one individually.   "One-thousand dollars for your help, sir and ten times more if you would be so kind as to give me a call if you should happen to see the woman, again, who filled out this application.   She is our lead witness who has disappeared.   Her family has hired me to find her and bring her home safely.   However, we have reason to believe she is armed and very dangerous.   I wouldn't approach her yourself."   Little Chief left a card on the coffee table next to the cash.   "Call me at that number should she return, and I will handle the rest.   And the ten grand cash will be yours as a finders fee paid for by her loving family."

Mr. Hernandez picked up the card, briefly looked at it and said,   "No problem."   After a hand shake, Little Chief was out the door and heading to his expensive looking Lincoln parked at curbside. As soon as he got into his car, he used his cell phone camera to shoot a picture of the application that Caroline had filled out.   After sending the photo to Trey, Little Chief called his brother asking for further instruction.   His reply was to hang back and see if any other information could be gathered in town. Knowing the woman in the video had a young child, Trey instructed his brother to check out all the schools in the area to see if any more information could be gleaned from a paper trail through the kid. Little Chief agreed and concluded the conversation. The photo that Trey had of Little El was blurred and very grainy.   Because the video surveillance camera was of low quality, the picture he took of her came out rather poorly.   But Trey sent the photo to Little Chief's cell phone anyhow, hoping to get lucky.

Chapter Eleven
Road Trip

Listening to El talk of everyday events while
on the road trip was like talking to a young adult,
Caroline mused.   She was so amazed as to how
acute her little girl was.   Of course, Mom and Dad
had a lot to do with it, teaching her the alphabet at a
young age, and moving right along to reading the
hard paged books, it didn't come as any surprise that
she would be the best in her class, and the only one in
her class to receive all A's on her report card.   But
still, it never failed to amaze Caroline to hear her
little daughter speak so fluently, sounding so much
more intelligent than others of her age group.   As
the trip went on, the girls talked about everything that
entered El's little sponge of a mind. They made a
good traveling pair as they drove for hours on the
first day.   Conversation and road games kept them
both entertained.   Long after dark, the two were still
enjoying the company of mom and daughter.   There
was no doubt that they shared a loving relationship.
Just as conversation was running dry, the singing
began.   El loved to sing like her Aunt Crystal.
Each time they would hear one of Crystal's songs on
the radio, no matter what they might be doing, the
two would stop and sing along.   A few hours into
the drive, Caroline could see that the van was quite a
gas guzzler.   Just before crossing over the first of
the big bridges outside of Pensacola from ward Basin

Rd. leading into Alabama, Caroline stopped for gas. At the station she checked the map for any campgrounds in the area.   She figured it would be much safer to stop at a registered campground to rest for the night than to be caught tired at a desolate truck stop should any trouble arise.   None too surprised, El became sleepy soon after getting gas. After making her bed in the back of the van, she was fast asleep, lulled by the sounds of the road and the traffic.   Caroline remembered a number of times when El was still an infant and reluctant to sleep, she and Jack had to put little El in her car seat and take her for a midnight drive just to get her to sleep.

Thinking about the good times with Jack kept Carline wide awake and eager to make the distance as short as possible.   With El fast asleep and plenty of 'unhealthy' energy drinks in the ice chest, Caroline was willing to do her best to travel as far as she could on the first leg of the trip.   Jack had once told her that the Live Oak Point bridge in Alabama was so long, it could be seen from space.   For some personal reason, Caroline took pleasure in crossing that bridge, it was more like a road of infinity. Straight into Mississippi, Caroline continued her travel undaunted by any signs of sleepiness. However, once she got to Covington, Louisiana, with the sun coming up at her back, she began to feel the sandman making his rounds, causing her fatigue and unable to continue any further.   Using the equipment in the van, she activated the navigation menu in the dash and requested information on the nearest campgrounds.   Within seconds, a location was acquired with directions at her fingertips.   After a job well done, with many miles behind them, Caroline was pleased to only have to travel another twenty minutes to find the campsite listed on the navigation device.   Seeing El so comfortable and sleeping deeply in the back of the van from the vantage of her rear view mirror, Caroline might have considered purchasing such a nice vehicle for days of travel had it not been so cumbersome and easy to spot.   Twenty minutes, give or take seventeen missing seconds, Caroline found the camping place via the voice activated navigation.   Soon after paying the park fees, she pulled into one of the campsites at the back of the park.   She backed the van into the parking place, allowing the front of the van to face forward for an easy and fast escape. Using her nifty little video camera, Caroline was able to set the surveillance to catch any car coming within five hundred feet of her van.   Knowing there was nothing but a thicket of woods behind her, she didn't concern herself with the rear of the van.   With the monitor place at the foot of her bed, she was able to see, at any given time, if anyone was approaching the van.   And the alarm on the monitor would alert her if any motion was detected within one-hundred feet. Odd as it was, Caroline felt safer and more secure traveling on the road than she did living in a house. Though Caroline was tired, she knew she would need to keep her strength up by eating more.   From within the shelter of the van, she used the stove to fry herself an egg.   After retrieving the mayo from the tiny fridge next to the sink, Caroline marveled as to how handy the van was working out to be.   She poured herself a drink and finished making herself a fried egg sandwich with lots of pepper.   Truly, she was impressed with the idea of, one day, buying a camper or van of her own.   After one last snack, she changed into comfortable clothes and snuggle along side her daughter.   As she began to drift off to sleep, she imagined herself shopping with Jack for a new motor-home.

Chapter Twelve
Florence 86 Boys

Big Mike was seventeen years old when Jimmy reappeared in the Florence 86 Boys' territory. Jimmy's biggest mistake wasn't having returned to town with the same old chip on his shoulder, but to have added insult to injury, Jimmy also decided to rob Mr. Washington's liquor store.   Making off with a sizable amount of cash and a bottle of Fireball whiskey, Jimmy had begun to spread the word that he was back, and with a vengeance.

At gunpoint, Jimmy showed no remorse stealing everything from the register and pistol whipping the man to the ground afterwards.   Many witnesses had seen exactly who was responsible for the attack.   It was as though, Jimmy didn't care. He was virtually leaving his calling card all over town, boasting his return and the fact that he was looking to settle a score with Big Mike. Unbeknown to him, since the day he left town two

years prior, Big mike had grown up quite a bit.   He
was hitting the weights like his brother Trey, and had
grown nearly eight inches.   His growing spurt
wasn't his only attribute befitting to his name, but his
skills were unmatched by any.   Big Mike had been
training with the best.   Street fighting had become
the sport of popularity.   Years before cage fighting
with the UFC ever existed, guys would gather after
hours in a gated parking lot of a auto shop, and sign
up to fight against contenders of equal weight.
Unlike the UFC, there were no rules other than no
weapons allowed.   The first guy to be knocked out
lost the fight, and no doubt, would be found there in
the parking lot the next morning.   That was how it
was done.   Big Mike was trained by his brother
Trey, and a black-belt expert in the art of Jujitsu.
Three times a week, Big Mike would train at the dojo
studying and practicing the art and philosophy of
Jujitsu, and then would hit the weights on the odd
days.   His dedication to the art of self-defense and
tactical fighting was exemplary to his peers.   Living
up to the name he was given, Big Mike turned out to
be an awesome contender in the ring.   At the
beginning of his fighting career, he might have lost
about twenty percent of his fights, which wasn't very
promising, but as he practiced and grew much
stronger and taller, his skills improved exponentially,
giving him the undefeated title he carried at the age
of seventeen.   Needless to say, his idol was Mike
Tyson who grew up on the same kind of streets with
the same laws of the jungle.   Widely respected
throughout the community, Big Mike and his family
would become a very powerful gang with ties across
the country.

      When word reached Big Mike that Jimmy
was back in town, looking for retribution, Big Mike
was only too happy to accommodate the man.   Only

one phone call was needed to send word that Big Mike was entering the ring against his childhood rival, and town bully.   Word traveled fast as Big Mike had announced the place and time.   *'West Florence Ave and South Vermont was the location -- the time was anytime after dark, just show up.'*   The streets lit up with the news that Big Mike was going to fight his old rival, who just happened to be the very same guy that robbed and beat down Mr. Washington.   With a festering anger already mounting against him, Jimmy would be running uphill and spinning his wheels if he was to gain any fans in his old town.   Streaming rumors claimed Jimmy must have had a death wish pitting himself against such a mad-dog fighter.   Not only had Big Mike been working on his fighting skills, but he had also been recruited to help with the family business. Ever since the event when Jimmy was exiled from town, Trey believed it was time for his little brother to start earning his way.   And equally so with all the new recruits, Big Mike got no preferential treatment. He started working with the big boys from the very start.   His weekly job was to help a small crew collect money for various services rendered, most of which was drug money.   It didn't take long before he learned just how the streets operated.   What Big Mike never knew was that most clients were, what most would call, *reluctant* to pay for protection for their, over priced, drugs.   More importantly, nearly eighty percent of those unwilling to pay were also ready, willing and prepared to fight for their freedom from their opposed obligation to work for the family - - the Florence 86 Boys.   Big Mike's initiation was a brutal awakening.   Like throwing a kid who had never the chance to learn to swim, into the deep end of the pool, Big Mike was pitted against some of the meanest and cruelest customers in the business.   It was Trey's orders that his brother be seen earning his right to his share absent of   any nepotism.   With nearly a half dozen fight or flight challenges on a daily basis, Trey's little brother learned the ropes fast.   He had little choice.   And like an enslaved and caged gladiator, Big Mike, slowly but surly, got mean and angry.   Identifying with the law of the jungle, he did his job successfully, and eventually earned his ticket to ride with the big boys.   But Trey had big plans for his little brother.   Unbeknown to Big Mike, Trey had a devious plan up his sleeve in store to toughen up his little brother.   Big Mike's right of passage was upon him, and Trey wasn't about to let anyone or anything get between his brother and the next step to official initiation.   The fact was, which Big Mike would never learn, was how Trey had searched out Jimmy and personally brought him back to town.   Big brother had big plans, giving little choice to Jimmy.   Trey told Jimmy the choices were quite simple; *'beat down Mr. Washington, rob the till and spread word that you are challenging Big Mike...or die.'*   Everyone knew never to disobey Trey.   Once marked by *the man*, you were had, and there was absolutely no hope for a reprieve.   And, of course, Jimmy knew Trey had no trouble finding him, so trying to run and hide, this time, would be impossible and futile.   Anticipating the kind of guy Jimmy was, the challenge was accepted with little hesitation.   Jimmy actually believed he had a chance to take Big Mike in the ring.

Who knows?   Maybe Trey was doing his little brother a lifelong favor.   Jimmy had always been Big Mike's thorn in his side, his nagging nemesis.   Once Trey was able to prove to Big Mike that Jimmy was just another guy, no better, no faster or stronger than he, Big Mike would finally come to realize that he truly was unbeatable and worthy of his name and rank in the family.   Just as Trey had been trained by his dad, Big Mike would be lessoned likewise by Trey, just as their father would approve or would have done had he still been alive.

Dusk would prevail as the light of day faded slowly with a crowd already gathering at the auto parts store, parking lot.   Only those involved in the fight and those who were family were actually allowed in the fenced parking lot.   The actual fight would be witnessed only by the closest members of the family.   Attending such matters of climbing rank had always been a traditional privilege.   Big Mike's right of passage was only minutes away from showdown.   As he showed up in his chopped and lowered 1963 Chevy Impala everyone came to learn that Big Mike was more than just ready for this day. He had trained hard and long for this victorious triumph.   In his mind, he had already won the fight. In his mind, he could already visualize Jimmy falling into an unconscious slumber.   Just as any fighter would psyche himself up for such a challenge, Big Mike exited his car, leaped over the fence and received a brief beating from his brother Trey, smacking Big Mike in face repeatedly.   The assault got Big Mike ready and angry.   The mean, mad-dog, anger festered deep in his soul.   And as he further prepared himself for the fight, stretching and jogging in place, he could hear the voices of his crew wondering if Jimmy would even show.   To Big Mike's chagrin, he too began to harbor doubts of Jimmy showing his face.   But seconds before orders were given to have him found, Jimmy was seen walking up the street acting brave and confident as ever before.   He lumbered his way over the fence and onto the parking lot.   The phalanxes of Trey's crew had encircled Big Mike as Jimmy approached. As Big Mike had his back to the challenger, members of the crew searched and frisked Jimmy for weapons.

"So, where is the faggot? Let's get this shit going." Reeking of attitude, whiskey and a childhood rancor no one could explain, Jimmy inquired, looking over the crowd.

No sooner had Big Mike turned around to face Jimmy, the crew granted access accordingly allowing the challenger to see just how much change had taken place over the past two short years. No doubt, Big Mike's eyes were the first to give his identity away. Aside from looking meaner and downright evil, he had a look of distain Jimmy had never before seen. Like two gun slingers facing off, they both showed their colors. Jimmy instantly flinched revealing his hesitation and shock to see how much change had taken place. Though it only took a fraction of a second for Jimmy to regain his aplomb, Big Mike detected the fear like a hungry, feral dog bearing down on his prey. He smelled the hesitation Jimmy tried desperately to hide.

Trey helped Big Mike remove his t-shirt. After a brief word no one but Big Mike could hear, Trey, then made an announcement to the crew, "This is Jimmy, as most of you already know. But what you may not know is this is the guy who beat down Mr. Washington at our corner market." Of course, everyone already knew that much, but Trey was using his tactics to boost an extra anger in his little brother. "Big Mike is going show all of you what we think of crack-heads who steal from the Florence 86 Boys and our commerce.

"Yeah, whatever…" Jimmy retorted, showing little respect for the formalities.

"Time to get busy, *Faggot.*" Big Mike announced as he threw the first left jab, connecting with Jimmy's jaw, knocking him three steps back into the crowd.

Answering with haste and contempt for Big Mike's family, Jimmy clambered to gain back his balance and attempted a right hook that was easily blocked and countered with another identical jab to Jimmy's jaw.   And again, Jimmy was throttled to the crowd behind.   As he was pushed back into play, he took a boxing stance, finally protecting his face from further attacks.

Big Mike faked another jab, launching a body blow to the gut of his opponent.   The combination to follow blasted Jimmy with two more body blows forcing Jimmy to drop his guard.   Big Mike saw the opening and took advantage with another jab to the jaw instantly followed by strong right uppercut.

Already, the blood was starting to stain Jimmy's teeth and lips.   At the corner of his mouth was a narrow stream of blood making it's way to his chin.   Jimmy was learning quickly just how outmatched he was.

"I have taken enough of your shit, Jimmy." Said Big Mike, throwing a powerful body blow once more, giving him another opening to the face.   Big Mike hadn't yet broken a sweat where Jimmy was already breathing heavy from the tempestuous body blows.

Showing relentless courage, Jimmy relied on his mean bullying ways to pursue the fight to the end. He made several attempts to find an opening, throwing a right to the face and missing.   Then, a left to the face, that was blocked.   Resorting to a body shot, Jimmy's attempt was quickly and skillfully answered with a counter that knocked Jimmy to the ground, dazed and whirring.   Instantly, he was raised to his feet by the crowd.   "You're nothing, faggot."   Jimmy brayed on.   "You've always been nothing, and you will always be nothing."

"Then do something about it, damn it.   And quit wasting my fucking time."   Big Mike cast his evil look that would have sent feral dogs off yipping in fear.

Jimmy made a good effort to charge Big Mike hoping to catch him off guard as he used to do back in grade school.   Looking much like the Superman Punch, Jimmy launched himself and all his weight forward, he attempted a plow into Big Mike's face. Had he connected, it might have been an effective assault.

With Big Mike's training and effective skill, he had already detected the telegraphed attack, and moved accordingly by shifting his weight to the side and allowing Jimmy to be lifted up of his feet and flipped over Big Mike's shoulder.   In Judo, this move is usually followed up with a crashing blow to the neck knocking out the opponent as Jimmy had landed on his back, crashing to the pavement.   No doubt, the impact was heard by every ear in the parking lot.   But Big Mike refrained from any follow through.   He had festered an ugly hatred for Jimmy for too many years to let him off so easily. Surely, knocking him unconscious at that point would have been an effortless task, but the effort was to teach Jimmy a lesson.   As soon as Jimmy got back to his feet, with help, Big Mike blasted a crashing right hook to Jimmy face, splattering blood in every direction.   As Jimmy wobbled and made his attempt to protect his face by keeping his guard, many more body blows would cause him to drop his heavy guard, leaving him open once again.   And each time the opening would reveal the mark, Big Mike would plant a powerful punch to the jaw, over and over again.   It was obvious after ten minutes into the fight, Jimmy was finished.   He had nothing left.   He could barely stand without help.   And yet, he persisted to spew his obscenities and vulgar disrespect for the neighborhood he grew up in. With a powerful spinning back kick, Big Mike launched the ultimate finale, blasting Jimmy backwards knocking him and five other guys off their feet.   A second later, Jimmy was still making an effort to rise to his feet.   It was a lost cause, he should have conceded, but his pride was too great to give in to futile efforts.   After another kick to the body, bones were heard cracking under the pressure of the kick.   Jimmy was spitting up blood and making no more attempts to get up, much less move. As Big Mike turned to get his shirt from his brother, he was faced off by Trey and everyone in the circle. It only took him a fraction of a second to understand what was expected of him.   As Trey stood cross-armed and adamant, Big Mike looked him in the eyes.

Trey answered with a tacit order of a skewed brow and a sidelong glance back at Jimmy who was face down, gurgling in a pool of his own blood.

In answer, Big Mike finished the job, making Jimmy his first kill.

Chapter Thirteen
Anticipation

It was a warranted, restful stop at the campsite where Caroline gathered about six hours sleep along side her little girl.   Without interruption or alarming alerts from her motion detector, the two girls rested well.   And just after noon with the sunny weather holding up, Caroline was back on the road, shortening the distance between them and Jack. Every mile traveled was that much closer to her man. Feeling more like a machine steadfast to accomplish a deemed goal, Caroline stuck close to the itinerary, making only the most necessary stops along the way. As Mom would point out each new city and state, El with her clever intellect would search the map to investigate how much closer they were.

The second day of travel brought them through Texas and halfway through New Mexico, before Caroline could travel no more.   Always being careful not to over-expend her abilities, Caroline located another camp to stop and rest-up. Conservation of just enough energy was in good order lest she fall asleep at the wheel.   But equally important, was the fact she would need to know her vigilant abilities were still intact to protect herself and El.   Caroline's protective nature stayed at the near-top of her list of priorities with a sharpened efficiency.   At no time, would she allow herself to drop her guard even to the smallest degree risking unforeseen dangers that seemed to lurk in the background of every turn.

Gaining a restful eight hours sleep on the second stop in Los Cruses, New Mexico, Caroline figured the third and final leg of the trip would bring the two of them to California and to the final destination of Calabasas where she and Jack had planned to meet.   Knowing that a meeting at the beach house would promote too many caged pheromones, Caroline thought it best to meet at mutual corners.   Though Caroline had explicitly instructed Jack to keep the announcement of her visit on the down-low, she wondered just how much she could trust Jack to keep his word in that department. Knowing how much Caroline loved Jack's family, it would be just like him to spark every emotion he could muster within her by making sure all her favorite people were in attendance at Pauly's estate on the hilltop.   Just thinking about Pauly, Roberto and Crystal gave her such a rush of emotions, she could barely contain herself.   A rushing chill of goose-bumps traveled the distance from the center of her shoulder blades to the nape of her neck, and on down to her fingertips each time she realized she was another state closer to her husband and loving family. Though it wasn't the proper time to give into the nagging dissonance that was playing havoc with her decision making, she wondered if she would have the strength to resist her man and be able to leave after the week long visit.   Subconsciously, she had already made many mental arrangements if such an occurrence arise.   Just for starters; all her cash and her favorite outfits were already packed in the van, making it easy for her to leave the rest of her, non necessary possessions behind.   The Jaguar and it's pink slip of ownership could be given to the landlord as payment for her breach of contract for not having given thirty days notice of intent to vacate.   Her only regret would be the loneliness she would be causing her boss, Fred Niedrickson who had grown so fond of her and Little Miss.

As the miles rolled on, and Caroline traveled ever closer, already imaging his smile, his touch and his wonderful, yet, obnoxitiously expensive cologne, her level of excitement would continue to rise for her husband and best friend, Jack.   Nearly kicking herself for not being strong enough to keep him from entering nearly all her thoughts, she would catch her mind rationalizing her reasons for staying in California.   Trying to drive safely and keep her mind occupied on the joy of reuniting with family and making sure she found Crystal feeling better, was her intention, when, each time, her horny disposition would have her squirming in the driver seat imagining how she might steal away with Jack and have her way with him.   *Jeez Louise, what is it with me?   Is Maxine's spirit haunting and possessing me?   Or is the vibration from the monstrous engine of this van having stimulating effects on me?*   Clearly, Caroline could feel the wetness pooling between her legs.   *Nope, this is all me.   Obviously, I'm a spineless, slutty, immoral, concubine in dire need of sex therapy or forty-eight and a half hours of complete privacy, most preferably with Jack, but not necessarily mandatory.   Good Lord, what am I going to do with myself?   Scratch that.   Never mind*

Once Caroline had reached Tucson, she was nearly crawling out of her skin with gripping anticipation.   Keeping to highway 10, Caroline made as few stops as possible.   The lively entertainment in the van consisted of El telling jokes and riddles she learned from school.

"Hey, I have a riddle for you…"   Mom declared.   "How far can El and Mommy travel into Arizona?"

El thought a moment.   "I don't know, Mommy.   How far?"

"Only half way onto Arizona."   Mommy answered, knowing El was having difficulty figuring the reasoning.

"Why only half way?"   Little El's tiny voice sounded so cute as she thought hard.

"Because, once you have already traveled halfway *into* Arizona, you would then be traveling the other halfway *out* of Arizona."

"That was a pretty good one Mommy."   El stated, as she noticed another of Crystal's songs playing over the radio.   "Can I?"   El questioned, indicating her desire to turn up the volume.

"Sure, sweetie."   Mom answered, already prepared to sing along with her daughter.

Jokes, riddles and singing was all they could do to keep from being attacked by overwhelming anxieties of excitement.   With every new city entered, El would pore over the map to see how many more inches (miles) were needed to travel to see her daddy.

Chapter Fourteen
Endometrial Malignancy

The results of the tests came back showing the same results as the first tests   taken.   It was an extremely painful and jousting reality that, thankfully, most don't have to face.   But in this case, Crystal was the one facing the horrors of her tenuous future.   After receiving the sad tidings, both she and Roberto consoled each other in an intrepid embrace.   It was time to prepare for a stout worthy battle.   After Roberto suggested yet a third opinion from another oncologist, Crystal refused to travel anymore.   She was weak and tired from both the disease that plagued her body and the traveling Roberto had insisted on in search of the truth.   Not that Crystal was willing to give-in to the potentially fatal diagnosis, she was merely preparing herself for the fight of her life.   Denial of her condition would, obviously, be a ludicrous mistake.   Though Roberto wasn't willing to admit to it, Crystal wasn't the least bit surprised by the onset of the disease.   She had been fighting with her condition nearly all her life. And though her gynecologist advised her against having any children, Crystal vehemently refused to listen.   It was her utmost desire to, one day, be able to bare a child.   When she was much younger, she had sustained a horrible injury precluding her from ever having children.   It wouldn't be until many years later, she would come to learn that not all her gestational female parts had been removed as the attending surgeon had claimed.   Perhaps it was an immaculate miracle or just a simple oversight on the doctor's part.   Either way, when Crystal found that there was even the smallest glimmer of hope to be offered, she shook off all warnings and prepared to be a loving mother.   And though every warning sign of danger came and passed as Crystal ignored all the advise of the medical profession, the news of her pregnancy, one day, had come to surprise and excite her and her husband to be.

The news of her pregnancy was the most elating she had heard in her entire life.   Though Roberto had no idea of the dangers she would face by refusing to abort the pregnancy, Crystal kept all the detriments and forewarnings to herself.   Her prenatal appointments were, for the most part, conducted in secrecy or privacy, so Roberto would never learn of the dangers that might take her life at the time of delivery.   It truly was a miracle that she was able to go full term as the time came nearer.   As it was, in the last two months, she had to be medicated to keep her from going into premature labor, as her body tried to reject the pregnancy.   But to her good fortune, luck had prevailed and the full term came to fruition with a beautiful baby girl to join the family.   Crystal was strong minded as she was physically strong with the will to see her little child grow up.   But fate still had a mighty hand in her future.   Soon after giving birth to Semorray, the damaging effects from her previous accident had caused her serious concern.   With severe endometriosis and first stage carcinoma, Crystal underwent a bilateral salpingo oophorectomy (complete removal of the uterus).   Crystal's mother was much younger than she when her mother had died from the same cancer.   Taking no risks, Roberto afforded all her needs making sure she wouldn't fall to the same fate as her mother.   But what Roberto wasn't willing to admit, Crystal had already understood that fate had other plans. Crystal's success for survival greatly hinged upon the hand of God and not the price tag on medical treatment or the cost of a good diet.

The young mother could not have been in better hands, but the tests results didn't discriminate will from capitulation, or rich from poor.   Crystal was diagnosed with the latter of stage three cervical cancer.   Even if she had already begun the therapeutic treatments of chemo, her chances of survival, according to several doctors, was less than thirty percent.   Only a miracle could save her now. Both Crystal and Roberto waited for the very last word of each doctor before telling the family of the unfortunate news.   Gianna was the first to be told the same evening the diagnoses was rendered.   She took it very hard, nearly squeezing the life out of

Crystal as she hugged her and responded with an ocean of tears.   The two girls had grown very close since Crystal and her dad first got together.   Though Gianna's biological mother was still alive and spent equal time with Gianna, the depth of love that she shared with Crystal was immeasurable.   The benefit of having a mother *and* a step mom was most fortunate, especially when both were on the same page as far as raising the child with love and wellbeing as the priority.   No doubt, Crystal was a loving parent divided equally among the two children.   Though Semorray was young and in need of extra care, Gianna knew how much Crystal loved her, and would do anything to protect her.   It wasn't long after she and Roberto got together that Gianna learned just how protective she was.   It was on the very night Crystal had decided it was time for a girl to girl talk to take place.   Inviting her step daughter, to be, out for ice cream seemed to be the appropriate place to have the talk.   It was Crystals intention to explain to Gianna just how much she loved her father.   Crystal wanted to be the one to tell the young girl that her father had proposed to her and she, first, wanted to know how Gianna felt before giving her answer.   It was a noble gesture to offer such a vulnerable young mind such as Gianna's. The sweet girl was very perceptive and approving from the start, but she felt especially honored to have Crystal ask how she felt about the idea.   Being treated and respected like an adult was very important to Gianna as Crystal had already perceived. But more importantly, Gianna knew just how much her father loved Crystal.   And knowing her father was happy was important to her as well.   Gianna had witnessed the marriage of her mother and father fall apart when she was young.   Ever since the divorce, she rarely got the chance to see her father smile or laugh.   He put up a good front when taking her to special places like Disneyland and such, but she knew how lonely he truly was.   It was, in fact, Gianna who first detected that there was a woman in her father's life when she saw the positive difference surfacing in his every actions.   He was quicker to smile than in the past, and she would catch him singing to the radio more often.   Little did she know, at the time, the woman he was dating was Crystal, the woman he was singing along with on the radio.   With her dad quick with a joke, or feeling less inhibited to laugh aloud, Gianna knew it was all due to a new woman in her father's life.

At the Ice Cream Parlor, were many of the kids would choose to get snacks and refreshments, Crystal and Gianna ordered two tall triple scoops on a waffle cone.   Many times over, Crystal had told Gianna that she was an old soul due to her ability to perceive the not so obvious in others.   And it was true.   Gianna   was very perceptive, with matters of family and others.   Crystal was truly impressed with her intuitive abilities.   As the girls laughed and spent girl time together, Crystal's main objective was to assure Daddy's young daughter that she would remain just as important to her daddy as ever before even if he was or was not to remarry.   It was, also, vitally important to Crystal to know that Gianna was in full acceptance of the marriage before they might move forward.   The young girl was a very intelligent and a very loving individual who's soul bled of kindness and consideration for others.   And though Crystal could have guessed there would be a favorable decision to come from Gianna, Crystal would never have been so bold or unfeeling not to show respect Gianna concerning such a sensitive subject matter.   Without delay or reservations of any kind, Gianna offered an overwhelming show of support toward Crystal and her dad's engagement proposal.   In celebration. Gianna toasted her ice Cream into Crystal's, mingling the odd flavors together, followed with laughter and excitement. The final outcome was quite an elating episode in Crystal's life.   The two happy girls were about to enter a new chapter in their life.   The jubilant mood seemed to escalate throughout the ice cream parlor as the volume of voices steadily got louder by the second.   The place was crowded with many teenagers and young adults; the kind of place to hang out with friends and first dates.   As the two girls talked passionately of future plans, weddings and the venue of Uncle Pauly's estate, an overt argument suddenly and violently broke out behind Giannas chair.   The young teenage boy seated directly behind Gianna chair had, for whatever reason, bolted from his chair and struck his girlfriend across the face with a crashing slap.   He smacked his date with such force, she had fallen from her chair into Gianna's side forcing her to fall as well.   Had it not been for Crystal's quick reflexes and foresight, Gianna could have been badly hurt.   But instead, Crystal leaped from her seat and intercepted the fall, cradling Gianna to safety.   With her adrenalin still on alert, Crystal placed Gianna safely out of harms way.   In an instant reflex, Crystal grabbed the retracted arm of the guy before he could fire another strike at his girlfriend's face who was already in tears and hurt from his first slap and the fall to the hard tiled floor. The timing couldn't have been more precise.   All the witnesses could see that the infuriated guy was not about to resist hitting her again.   Who's to say how badly the poor girl might have been hurt had it not been for Crystal's interception when she grabbed his arm and wrestled him to equal resistance, stopping him flat in his tracks? who's to say how badly the poor girl might have fared.

"Let go of me, bitch, or I might have to show you and your little sister some lessons too." Hollered the angry boy, tugging and pulling to free his arm from Crystal's unrelenting grip.

An instant hush fell over the parlor as everyone in the place could clearly see and hear the tussle unfolding before them.

The intolerant anger in Crystal's eyes was instantly perceived by the boy who was dressed in tight pants and a Levi jacket.   "I dare you…" Crystal drawled, staring him down.

"Dare me to what?   Hit you?   I just might!" The boy said, trying to retain his tough act in front of his peers and tearful girlfriend.   The boy had no idea what he was up against.

"Stop flapping your jaw and do it already." Shouted Crystal, as she violently pulled at his arm, tipping him off balance.

"Your lucky I don't pound you into next Tuesday, you stupid, psycho bitch."

"Are you a complete moron, boy?   I am begging you to hit me.   Now get to it.   Hit me! Show me what you've got."   Crystal was fuming with anger, glowing of seething eyes and reeking of brimstone.

The boy hesitated to speak at first.   The fear in his face was registering an obvious retreat. "You're nuts lady.   I--"

The silence in the ice cream parlor was near deafening.   Even the incessant ring of the cash register had suddenly come to a halt as the hard-working clerks stopped scooping to see what was happening.

"I didn't think so.   You're a coward.   A cowardice little pea of a man is all you are…" Crystal interpreted, announcing loud enough for all to hear.   "You beat on weaker people because you are too indecisive.   You are mad at the world because you haven't the guts to come out of the closet. Have you told your momma you are gay?"   A hush of chuckling whispers could barely be heard in the background as Crystal continued her insulting rant. "Your affliction is so obvious.   Look at you with your Justin Beiber haircut and pants so tight, it's no wonder your falsetto voice hasn't changed yet. Dare I ask if your balls have dropped yet?"   Crystal said, still waiting for him to grow a spine and attempt to hit her.

"Now listen lady.   I've had--"

"No you listen, Peter Pan."   Crystal shouted in his face, never once letting lose of his arm, jerking him with nearly ever other syllable.   "I couldn't care less about your sexual preferences, Dorothy.   If this girl on the floor here is too stupid to leave you because you keep using her as your personal punching bag, that's her problem.   But when your insipid, childish tantrum injures my little girl with this chair, that's when draw the line.   And you clearly crossed that line, Peter Beiber.   Now, the way I see it, you have one of two choices.   You either leave here after helping this young lady to her feet without any more of your insipid comments, *or* I pound your creepy haircut into next year, and call the cops to have your carcass hauled away.   Just nod your head, princess…do you feel me?"   Nearly snarling every word, Crystal finally released his arm.

In reply, the boy said nothing as he tried to hide his eyes from the patrons in the parlor.   After helping the girl to her feet, he left the establishment as advised.

The girl he helped to her feet was the first to incite the applause that got the entire parlor to chime in.

Before Crystal had the chance to cool her engines, one of the clerks from behind the counter had already replaced Gianna's ice cream that had fallen to the ground. "One scoop of lemon sorbet, one blue raspberry sorbet and one bubble gum, on the house. Compliments of all us envious girls wishing we had the guts to do what you just did." The pretty young girl announced as she handed Gianni the triple scoop and then offered an extra applause to Crystal.

No doubt, Gianna understood she was in good hands when she was with her new step mom to be.

Chapter Fifteen
Making arrangements

Roberto and Crystal had made a special trip to Calabasas to alert his dad of the situation. Pauly knew the unscheduled visitation must have been of bad tidings inasmuch as the couple had never before made such an effort to speak frankly in person. The stifling news of Crystal's condition hit everyone tragically hard.   Pauly, the big tough man who was capable of eating roofing-nails for breakfast, broke down in tears and sat on his office couch, burying his head in his hands.   It was as though the man was reliving his past all over again.   His sadness was amplified by knowing how much Roberto loved his wife.   Pauly couldn't bear to think how miserable his son will be if a miracle wasn't attained and implemented soon.   It was no secret that Crystal played a vital role in the family's affairs.   Second hub to Pauly, she was the staple filter that would handle family matters before they reached Pauly.   If there was a way to mollify a situation before causing Pauly any stress, Crystal was the one to create that calm and seek better avenues for family business. Though Crystal operated two very large companies, she was never too busy to help the family.   Since the day of her wedding, Pauly swore that she had married the entire family.   Taking her under his wing, Pauly showed her the ropes of the business.   He knew exactly what Crystal was made of, taking confidence in her abilities as the family matriarch.   Gutsy and not the least bit squeamish, Crystal accepted the honor proudly.   She had the kind of personality, one could not help falling in love with.

It was no wonder when Anthony Betuchelli worked his way up the ranks of the family business, he would take a turn for the worst.   Anthony, better known as Tony, was what Pauly referred to as a hot head; too eager to jump the gun and make the wrong choices out of hostility and anger.   Though he was a hard worker and did what he was told, for the most part, Pauly was able to read between the lines. When Tony chose to flash a gun instead of using logic and reason at one of the family business job sights, Pauly had suggested he be demoted to a lesser sensitive job lest he hurt someone, if not get himself killed.   But is was Crystal who was able to pacify the situation and call a truce between the two men. Putting Tony on a probationary basis, he was able to keep his present position with the business provided he could prove his ability to manage his hot, Italian anger.   Tony agreed, promising to keep himself in line.   The probation period was six months. Unfortunately, for Tony, as it turned out, the six months was far too long for him to handle.   Tony never grasped the idea of diplomacy and eloquence that the family fondly pursued with all business matters, including the collections department.   Pauly had always made it clear to Tony that they had qualified muscle for the clients that resisted making proper payments.   It wasn't his job to throw his weight around, or in this case, a gun.   Just six weeks into his probation, Tony got angry with a client who refused to make a full payment.   Out of a fit of rage, Tony pulled a gun and placed it to the man's temple, forcing the man to the ground.   The client had a history of being a pain in the ass with an attitude to amplify matters tenfold.   But it didn't give Tony the right to disobey Pauly's strict orders of hierarchy. The tussle between Tony and the client became a family embarrassment when the gun went off amid the wrestling entanglement on the floor of the man's apartment.   The bullet passed through the apartment's dividing wall into a family's home on the other side.   A young boy was struck in the leg with a superficial wound.   Thankfully, the police who took the call, contacted Pauly immediately.   By offering the family of the young boy a rather large sum of money, the police were able to mediate the situation and alleviate the hassling need for a police report and the District Attorney's involvement.   Of course, the cop received a sizable compensation as well.

Fortunately, Crystal's beauty and eloquence was able to make the problem go away for Pauly and the family.   But the unfortunate problem with Tony still existed.   Then he was removed from the fieldwork of his preference.   He felt wronged and passed over. The young man of twenty-six felt he was personally attacked and wronged by the family.   His reasoning was obviously misguided by his inability to manage his emotions.   Several times, he attempted to meet up with Pauly, unannounced or invited, at the Calabasas estate.   There was one very important rule that Pauly had made clear to all the family members, and that was to call for an appointment before making a surprise appearance.   Immediate family, were the only members allowed to bend the rules. But Tony continued to defy the rules of the business until one day, Pauly had to make the critical choice to place Tony at a menial job with one of the family restaurants.   Pauly had, several times, told Crystal that Tony should be grateful he wasn't dropped off in Siberia without a sweater or shoes for the way he was behaving.   But the truth be told, Crystal knew exactly what Pauly would have done had it not been for her pacifying mediation.   And it wouldn't have been as pleasant as a one way ticket to Siberia, that was for certain.   Tony was given strict instruction to wait a year before showing his face around the family, giving Pauly time to enough to cool off. Tony wasn't pleased as he offered a few choice carnal verbs that, fortunately for him, didn't reach Pauly's ears.   In a sense, Crystal had literally saved Tony's life.   The trouble he had caused the family wasn't worth the popularity it was earning.   But that was Crystal's way.   And Pauly loved her all the more for being the understanding woman she was. Further proving Crystal's family honor was the fact that Pauly was fully aware of Tony's intentions with

Crystal.   The young man was quite taken with
Crystal.   Of course, Crystal never once let on.   She
made her opinion very clear at every turn and
opportunity.   However, Tony's stubborn pride and
arrogance never letup.   No doubt, his major
downfall was his inability to accept his failures and
move on.   Oddly, in his own distorted way of
thinking, he actually believed that Crystal was fond
of him, only playing hard to get.   After his transfer
to the restaurant, Tony was given a lesson in
relationships and etiquette.   Unbeknown to Crystal,
who would not have approved, Pauly made the call
that put the muscle on Tony.   It was only a warning,
but persuasive just the same.

The idea of watching Crystal wither away in
the months to come much like his beloved wife,
drove Pauly crazy with sadness and indignation.
After the go-rounds, with Pauly making every
suggestion under the sun for Crystal to try, Roberto
had assured him that all the attempts had already
been made more than once.   Pauly could see that the
two had been very thorough with the management of
her illness.   No leaf had gone unturned.   And that
was when Pauly knew he had no other choice but to
pull the ace out of his sleeve.   It was an option he
never thought he would have sought.   He wasn't
even certain how to go about meeting with the
contact, but he made it his mission to save Crystal's
life.   He might not have had such an option back
when his wife was sick with Cancer, but he damn
well would make it his job to exercise the option this
time.   Pauly picked up his office phone and dialed.
After a brief discussion, Pauly was pleased to find
that he had discovered options that only needed a
time and date for confirmation.   He hung up the
phone and offered a wholesome smile.   "Are you up

for travel?"   Pauly asked Crystal, with earnest intent on his mind.

"How far are we talking, Pauly?"   Crystal understood he had a plan.   He wouldn't have bothered to bring it up if it wasn't a viable avenue to take.

"Several hours."   Pauly was being as pragmatic and frank as possible.

"By car or plane?"   Roberto inquired, wondering where his father was talking about traveling.

"Nixon Nevada, by car."   Pauly said, sounding more adamant than ever before.

Crystal looked to Roberto with a vote of confidence.   "I think I can handle it, baby." Crystal said confidently.   She knew her limitations.

"Are you certain we couldn't fly, dad?" Roberto knew that traveling by car, that far, would be hell on her condition.

"It's uncharted territory, and we have no jurisdiction.   We will need to bring the troops and the muscle for her protection."   Pauly said with a mysterious note to his calm.

Roberto knew exactly what Pauly was saying. Uncharted was something the family would rarely risk, and having no jurisdiction meant they would have no political back up should things go wrong. For Pauly to take a such a risk meant just how much Pauly was willing to put on the line for Crystal's life. "If you feel there is an honest chance to beat this cancer, I would be willing to carry her on my back to get her there.   But I'm going to need a little intel, dad.   I have never even heard of Nixon Nevada. What would we be seeking there?"   Roberto truly would have done anything for Crystal.   Nothing was more important to him than family.

Pauly knew he would eventually need to

explain himself.   As the question was brought up, Pauly walked to his desk where he opened a drawer of his many files.   From the depth of documents and private information came a file with Crystal's name on it.   It was the very file that Pauly had initiated when Roberto first started dating Crystal many years before.   Just like when Jack started dating Caroline, Pauly had initiated an investigation to learn all that needed to be known about her and her past. Business and safety depended on such stringent security measures.   And now, it was time to reveal some facts that Pauly had never before mentioned to anyone.   "As you know, Crystal, it is protocol to do a background check on all our newer family members.   And when I did some digging into your friends at the Shot of Gold I was very intrigued, to say the least.   I don't know if your friend Mike ever mentioned it to you but he is a Free Mason among other things.   *Both Roberto and Crystal had a very deep past with Mike and his wife Miranda.   They owned a night club called the Shot of Gold where the couples had spent many dinners and dancing together.   For all intensive purposes, Mike and Miranda were family to Roberto and Crystal.   They possessed a bond that traveled back through lifetimes of history.*

"He never mentioned being so, but what does that have to do with your research?"   Crystal said, wondering how Mike would somehow be involved in such matters.

"It appears to be a very long story.   In fact, it wasn't until I read some of his books long ago that I learned just how involved he is with the supernatural way of things, which I'm sure you are fully aware of. In his books he speaks very highly of you."

Crystal smiled tentatively.   "I've read his books.   He's a very talented writer."   Crystal said with hesitation, wondering what Pauly was hedging at.

"He's more than just a writer, Crystal." Pauly looked to Roberto and Crystal with a pause of reverence.   The man is a Shaman."

Pensively, Crystal looked at Roberto and back at Pauly.   "Mike Shane?   The guy who found his own long lost time capsule and used the money he discovered to open a night club is also a Shaman? You got the right guy?"

"It shouldn't be that hard for you to understand the possibility.   After all, he's entrenched with a family of mediums and spiritualist that tap into uncharted depths."   Pauly reasoned.

"That much is true, but I was never made aware of his being a Shaman."   Searching her mind for data, she asked,   "Isn't that a spiritual healer, like a medicine man of the American Indian?"

Pauly raised an eyebrow and nodded in answer.

"An you believe he can heal me?"   Crystal had her doubts about Pauly's investigation's findings.

"It wouldn't be Mike in the physical form actually."   Pauly tried to put it into proper terms without sounding completely insane.

"Dad, what are you talking about?"   Roberto was feeling confused and growing concerned for his father's mental health.

"It's a long story, but if your read his books starting with the first one published called '*Love Returns Through The Portal of Time*' you will find that he speaks of a past life episode."   Pauly explained further.

"Yes, I remember…the witch trials and the young boy named Jason and so on…"   Crystal could have recited the book verbatim, she had read it so many times.

"Well, I know this may sound crazy, but bare with me here.   Jason Mathison and Mike Shane are one in the same."

Crystal looked at Pauly with a look of humor and curiosity combined as she shook her head. "Yes, I know that.   I read the books.   All of them. He has recited many past lives."

"That's just the point, Crystal.   Pauly leaned forward and stood up from his desk.   With the file still in his hand, Pauly walked from behind his desk to join the kids on the couch.   Placing the file in Crystal's lap, open to several photographs, Pauly sat next to Crystal.   "Do you recognize this guy?" Pointing to the photo, Pauly already could have guessed the answer.

"I can't say that I do."   After looking closely, she noticed the burn scars on the man. "However, he has the same scars as Mike."   She looked closely at the photo.

"Bingo!"   Pauly announced with better clarification.

"Pauly, you aren't making any sense to me. Who is this guy?"   Crystal hadn't put it together only because she, just like Pauly and most of the deep thinkers on Earth, couldn't believe in the possibility. No one in there right mind would believe in such mysteries.   *Only a native American Indian could fathom such magic because their philosophy and culture encounters such thought on a daily basis. The fact is, only the native Americans are capable of understanding the nature of human beings.   And only they have the respect for Mother Earth that allows their beliefs to walk the path together in harmony.*

He's Jason Mathison."   Pauly reported. The photo was a copy of an old picture taken some time in the 1800's.   Then Pauly removed the top photo, revealing the one beneath.

It didn't take long before crystal was able to guess who the woman was in the photo that stood along side Jason.   "This must be his wife Ceenatanee."   Looking closer at the photo copy, Crystal remarked, "And she's just as beautiful as Mike described her to be in his books.   But I still don't understand the connection you are driving at, Pauly."

"Keep turning the pages of each of those pictures, Crystal, and take notice of the dates at the bottom of each photo."   Pauly instructed, showing a strong hint to the answers that, so far, had alluded her.

Crystal turned the next page, where it showed Jason standing at the grave sight of his wife. Clearly, the books had stated that Jason had lived out his life with Ceenatanee through to her ninety second year of life.   It was also understood that Jason died just months after.   But the photo copy was contradictory to the facts that Mike wrote and told about.   In the photo, Jason looked to be in his early thirties.   "This makes little sense to me.   Are these real?   You know there are professionals who fake photos just like these for a living and a small fortune."   Crystal was the kind who would doubt her own eyes rather than believe in magic, insisting that magic was nothing more than smoke and mirrors incited by naive imaginations.

"That's Jason Mathison.   I can *guarantee* it." His adamant words struck Crystal with an impact of loss for words.   "Keep turning the pages."   Pauly encouraged her on.

The next photo was taken nearly fifty years later.   The date at the bottom of the page documented the chronological stage of history. With the turn of the next page, Crystal was showing a flustering doubt.   "This is impossible.   People don't live to be over a hundred years old without showing so much as a gray hair."   Barked Crystal.

"Actually, he was born in 1813, sweetie." Pauly said, hedging once again.

"And he lived to be how old?"   Crystal had no idea what Pauly was about to reveal to her.

"Turn the next page and see for yourself" Instructed Pauly.

The date showed 2007, with Jason looking identical with all the other photos.   "I don't believe this."   Crystal rejected the evidence.

"My own P. I. took that photo in 2007.   I didn't believe it myself, at first.   But the fact remains, that's Jason Mathison in the flesh, and he still lives to this day.

"And I'm to believe he is over two-hundred years old, and still looking like he just stepped out of his fifteen year high school reunion?"

"Pretty much…yeah."   Pauly answered frankly.

"Okay, so lets say that I buy into all this craziness, which I surely don't, Pauly.   What has this to do with me and Nixon Nevada?"

"As you might   remember in those books that your friend Mike wrote, Jason Matheson had the healing touch to cure all types of ailments…"

"Yes, but he never mentioned a malignant cancer that can't be touched or cured topically." Crystal reasoned with patience running thin and more questions welling to the brim.

"That is true.   What I found out is that Mike wasn't revealing the entire truth about his abilities in those books of his.   After reading between the lines, I found that medical history dates back to an endless barrage of inhumane medical practices that nearly always resulted in certain death of the patient.

However, in Jason Mathison's case, the documented medical files proved a series of miracle cures dating all the way up until his disappearance.   With the onslaught of politics and his overwhelming popularity, I can only figure, the man went into hiding to save his own soul."   Pauly attempted to reason with factual evidence.

"But *you* managed to find him."   Crystal implied a notion of serendipity.

"You don't want to know what this investigation cost me.   For nearly two years, this Jason Mathison had become my hobby, intrigue and preoccupation.   Just to quench my own curiosity I *had* to investigate this guy further.   You of all people, knowing this Mike guy as well as you do, I would think this information would be easy for your to swallow."   Pauly said feeling disappointed.

"It's not like swallowing an aspirin, Pauly.   I have always believed in Mike's stories and Miranda's psychic abilities.   It is true, I have seen things even you wouldn't believe, but the strangeness behind a man who is two decades old with the ability to cure cancer?   I would think his name would be in all the tabloids as often as aliens and Sasquatch."   Crystal's reasoning made perfect sense to both Pauly and Roberto.

That was when Pauly opened the other file that was on Crystal's lap.   Just as she had predicted, was a popular tabloid of a man who was struck by lightening and lived. But later discovered that he had the miracle blood to cure any illness.   The tabloid showed that the FBI was offering a twenty-five thousand dollar reward for information leading to his capture and conviction for having robbed and murdered a couple at a motel.

"That makes perfect sense…a guy who could buy the state of New York with his curing abilities would rob and kill for no reason other than to allow the FBI to issue a warrant for his arrest.   So far, this is the only thing that makes sense to me."   Crystal announced.

Roberto took the paper from Crystal as he was reading on about the details of the case involving the man who was struck by lightning.   "Look here babe."   Roberto said, seeking her attention.   "This lightning guy is said to have the same blood properties as Jason Mathison.   I remember reading about this story.   The reward eventually reached one-hundred thousand dollars, when one day, the papers said, the lightning guy and his wife were killed by the FBI.   It actually makes perfect sense."   Roberto was putting the pieces of the puzzle together as they would formulate in his mind.

"I'm glad somebody sees the light."   Crystal rebutted.

"Think about it.   The paper says everything that my dad had found to be true as well.   Mathison disappears when demand for his magical blood becomes too great to handle.   This Jackson guy who was struck by lightning is also discovered to have this miracle blood and disappears when the, so called, "government" tried to put the lid on him and his abilities.   Down here," Roberto pointed out the continued story on the back page. "the medical jargon states that this kind of blood is so rare that it only exists in one person per one-billion.   The very fact the FBI had such an interest in him indicates to me this is the real thing.

Crystal wasn't completely sold by the story. "But this is just a silly tabloid.   Are we the men in black now?"

Then Pauly showed one last picture to the kids.   It was a photo taken by his P.I. just a year before.   The photo was a candid shot of Simon

Jackson, the guy struck by lightning, and Jason Mathison enjoying a leisure day on, what looked to be, a horse ranch in Napa Valley, California.   The bottom of the color photo showed the date and address of the site.

"So, how does this connect with a Shaman, Freemasons and Nixon, Nevada?"   Sounding more like a lead to a joke, Crystal asked for the pertinence with desperation in her voice.   Wanting more than anything to be cured of her death sentence, she was willing to believe in most anything, as long as it wasn't so far fetched that even a child could see through the holes in the story.

"My Freemason brothers are merely waiting for a phone call form me to confirm our arrival at the Indian reservation in Nixon, Nevada.   That's were we will be meeting with what the Indians call the Shaman who is Jason Mathison."   Pauly reported with determination.

Crystal's jaw nearly hit the floor.   "You were able to set up a meeting with this two century old guy?   For me?"

"If anyone could pull off something like this it would be my dad."   Roberto stood up to hug his dad.   "How certain are you about his abilities to cure such an advanced case of cancer?"   Roberto felt the same hesitation to show any excitement just yet. Getting one's hopes up could be far more detrimental than just accepting one's destiny and preparing for it.

"I have done a lot of research on the matter. Never did I think it would be necessary for any one of us to use.   But my own curiosity caused me to look quite critically at the facts.   I have to tell you, Bobby.   It is more than just promising.   I would never have brought it up if I didn't think it actually had promise."   The tears began to well up in Pauly's eyes.   "If I had known about this guy twenty just years ago…"

"I know, dad."   Roberto consoled his father who was having trouble with his overwhelming emotions.

"I can't let this happen to Crystal too, Bobby."   Pauly began to cry aloud.   "I love her like my own daughter.   This is so unfair."   Pauly sobbed showing little restrain, allowing the tears to stream down his face.

Roberto held his father tightly in his embrace allowing him to release his emotions.   "I know, dad. God willing, this Shaman guy will make it right."

The tears this man shed were for both his wife and for Crystal, the two most dearest and important women in his life.

Chapter Sixteen
Travel Arrangements

Pauly made the second urgent call to his

associates.   Arrangements with the Freemasons were made.   Large sums of money were wired. And the troops were rounded up for a very long road trip.   It was fully understood that without the reinforcements of the troops in uncharted territory would be certain suicide.   With Crystal being critically ill, it was all the more reason to take extra precaution while away from the fortress of the estate. Roberto made the arrangements to have the customary, bullet-proof limousines delivered to the house.   A caravan of six long black limousines were rented for the trip.   Roberto tried to make the trek as comfortable as possible for his wife who's condition was worsening by the day.   She had already lost nearly ten pounds in the past eleven weeks.   She hadn't been able to work at either of her businesses for over five months.   Crystal was fighting the battle of her life.   Her bravery would never have had you guessing that she was sick in the least.

Gianna and Semorray were made to stay behind with family under heavy guard at the estate in Calabasas.   While on the road in transit it would be far too difficult for the family to protect the children should a firefight break out.   The history of such attacks speak for themselves.

Within twenty-four hours, half of the convoy was already in rout to meet with the other half.   As a precautionary measure of security, Pauly and all the limousines packed with munitions and food supplies left from the estate first as the first heat.   While in rout, the second heat met up with the first at a designated location, never stopping to give away anyone's identity.   Once the convoy was onward to Nevada, there was nearly forty-five cars in attendance, with more to join later at the Nevada border.

Equally similar to the procedures of the Secret

Service while protecting the president, there were no obvious markings on any of the limousines indicating which car was occupied by the main family members. Pauly's men had also trained in the field with such vehicles.   They were well versed with tactical driving skills to evade the enemy, and protect the occupants.   At any given moment, the, well paid, drivers were fully prepared to put their lives on the line as they were hired to do.   Many of Pauly's crew were members from the old country where many battles had been fought and won.   The experience these men gained from the field was used as valuable training tools for the novice, younger drivers.   Many of these drivers may only be called upon six or eight times a year for their expertise services, but the pay from this adjunct job, most times, exceeded their annual pay scale from their main job, making Pauly's crew very loyal and dependable.

The history of armored cars became a serious industry back in 1927 when a makeshift armored vehicle was destroyed by a simple explosive, allowing the attackers to make off with over a hundred thousand dollars cash that was entrusted to the company of the armored car.   Since the industry first started, every attack of each generation of armored cars had become a learning process on what to do better.   To date, there are less than twenty different companies that specialize in such protections.   Most people wouldn't know it but there are thousands of cars on the road every day that are fully protected with armored technology, and yet, you wouldn't know it because each one is prided by the fact the protection is totally undetectable, making the vehicle far more desirable to the customer.   One company known as Alpines Armory Inc. has designed several levels of protection creating a large market of desired technology.   Jack had his crew trained directly with the company that rents the limousines inasmuch as they are best qualified to help the drivers understand the custom design and requirements of each car.   The limousine is approximately fifteen hundred pounds heavier than a standard one of his likeness without armor, therefore brakes and suspension are beefed up to accommodate the safety of operation.   The level of protection has come a long way since the twenties.   The science today uses various materials in addition to the heavy steel construction of the past.   Composites have become the leading materials used now because they are much lighter in weight and are actually stronger than steel.   Ballistic Nylon is one material used, another is polyethylene fiber, and also, Kevlar blankets.   When layered, these combinations of materials are virtually impenetrable by armor piercing rounds traveling at nineteen-hundred miles per hour, well over two and a half times the speed of sound.   Even the glass of the vehicle is replaced with plastics that are several inches thick and able to absorb the bullets that might be used in an attack. Various kinds of people use these highly protected vehicles, from politicians and celebrities to corporate moguls.   Leonardo Davinici, back in 1485, drew a crude design of the first armored vehicle that was similar to a saucer shape with a three-hundred sixty degree firing range.   No doubt, the ideas and technology has come a long way since.   And the rental of such vehicles is quite reasonable considering the need.

      While in the privacy of the back portion of the limousine, behind protective glass, Roberto, Pauly and Crystal made the best of the long trip.   During the first hour, Crystal slept as she prepared for the long journey.   Rest, ostensibly, became her only refuge from pain, incessant fatigue and discomfort. As she drifted in and out of sleep, she silently listened to the boys' discussion with half an ear. Roberto was elated to be making the trip, and was looking forward to meeting with Jason Mathison. Back when the FBI was attempting to locate Simon Jackson, Roberto had been attentively keeping track of the progress of the investigation, much like half the nation, at the time.   It was a magical emotion evoked in every individual who pondered the idea of being cured of every and any disease on the planet. Rumor of the many tabloids had hinted that the immortality of the carriers of said blood type had no limitations, and no known life cycle.   And after seeing the photos of Jason at the age of two-hundred, it was no wonder the government wanted to capture and control the people who possessed such unique blood types.   And it was no wonder the Free Mason's had much to do with the protected secrecy of the matter and those involved.   Pauly and Roberto had never before realized that their interests in such matters were so similar.   When Roberto spoke of Mike Shane's family and their supernatural abilities, the two seemed to become entranced by discussion of the topics and all the ramifications that it implied.   Roberto had supplied his dad with fantastic stories that he, himself, had witnessed and that no one would have guessed possible.   The intrigue was both fascinating and mind boggling. Roberto told a story of a girl named Destiny who, due to a rare disease, eventually lost her vision.   But the story went on to describe how her paranormal abilities increased exponentially as her blindness became certain and accepted.   By way of a psychic technique, Destiny was able to use her gift by touching items that had been owned or touched by certain individuals.   Once she was able to touch the item, she literally could sense the presence, character and actions of the other person.   Even if the other person had died long before, Destiny could tell you most anything about that person.   Roberto went on to describe how Destiny worked with Crystal at her insurance company, and was able to retrieve information from a simple piece of paper that was touched by a criminal for only a brief time.   Using the information she learned from the paper, Destiny had solved a crime that was committed by the guy months earlier.   The man was eventually convicted of his crimes and sent to prison.   Pauly was astounded that his kids hadn't spoken of such things before.   He seemed to be acting like a young child, totally enthralled by the stories Roberto would described.

"Quite frankly, dad.   I never would have guessed that you had an interest in the supernatural, much less believed in such strange events."   Roberto said, feeling amazed he and his dad had such similar interests.

"It wasn't until I moved to the states that learned about such matters.   Especially when this Simon Jackson guy made headlines.   When I made the connection between the two, I was convinced of it's validity.   I had to search out the truth to find out more."

"And thank God, you did."   Both Roberto and his dad kissed the cross they wore around their necks.

"I'm somewhat surprised this Mike fellow never told Crystal of his relationship to Jason Mathison."   Pauly inquired.

"Knowing Mike Shane as well as I do, I believe he has good reason for that.   He was probably fully aware of the can of worms he would be opening had word gotten out."   Roberto reasoned.   "I for one, would not have told a soul if I had that kind of gift."

"I suppose not, but I feel it was a shame that he had allowed his sister Destiny to go blind without offering any help."   Pauly said, trying to see reason for such a selfish action.

"Perhaps, but I believe Mike was able to see beyond his sister's handicap.   Mike is no fool.   His reason for the course of action that he takes on a daily basis has many consequences.   I have a strong suspicion that his gift is far stronger than anyone of us could possibly suspect or even begin to understand.   For reasons that go beyond time itself, Mike has to make hard choices.   His sister's journey is, no doubt, preordained.   If it was meant for her to live out her life in total blindness, I figure Mike knew what he was doing by not intervening.   The very that fact a criminal who murdered his own wife and possibly others is living out his live in prison because Destiny was able to see his actions through her expanded psychic abilities, leads me to believe he had done exactly what was meant to be.   Quite frankly, I don't see Destiny as a mournful or pessimistic person due to her handicap.   I have met with her and spoken with her many times.   And aside from being a very lovely person, I have always seen her smiling and happy, never looking at the glass half empty.   She looks at her blindness as a gift rather than an inhibiting factor in her life.   She has a great man in her life who has asked for her hand in marriage, and I honestly believe she couldn't be happier.   Truly, there is more to the story than what was written on the pages of his books.   I have to say that I am quite impressed and intrigued by his talents."   Roberto stopped just short of one understanding.   "What I can't make any sense of is the relationship between him and Jason Mathison.

When you read the reports on him, how did you figure that he was the same person when clearly, they look nothing alike in the photos?   Do you suppose they are twins…the kind that are not identical?" Roberto's inquiry made for a challenging discussion.

Pauly thought about his answer carefully. He too, seemed to be at a loss for the right equation. "I haven't quite figured that out either.   I thought perhaps, you would be able to help me with that one."   Pauly said, feeling sadly discouraged.

"Men…everything has to be written out in black and white, and spelled out with explicit instructions and pictorial directions or they wouldn't be able to think for themselves.   How is it you two Neanderthals even remember to breathe?"   Crystal quipped, coming out of her sleepy slumber as she sat herself up in the seat.

"Firstly, you are forgetting that I am in car with you two.   If you choose to talk using such big words, at least try to take a breath between sentences so I can get my remedial brain to catch up."   Pauly teased.

"So explain the obvious to us, because I am dying to hear your view on the matter."   Roberto stated, looking to be genuinely interested in the matter.

Crystal straightened herself up in the seat, straitening her blouse, and rubbed the fog from her eyes. "If you took notes when you read the books Mike wrote, you might have found that he refers to the life spirit on each lifetime through reincarnated lives as the soul."

Both Roberto and Pauly nodded in agreement.

"So it stands to reason that Mike and Jason are, somehow, sharing the same soul."

"Is that even possible?"   Pauly said, showing doubt.   "Is there really such a thing?"

Crystal reached to her back pocket and retrieved her cell phone.   'If I'm not mistaken, the term for a shared soul is called a 'Twin Flame'. Usually, it is one male and one female who share a soul, but I guess, in this case, perhaps there are four." Crystal tapped at a few keys on her phone to access the internet.   Sure enough, she found a site that refers to Twin Flames, sometimes called Twin Soul. Crystal read aloud the definition of what many believe to be the shared soul theory.   As far back as 2500 years ago, Plato once wrote;   *"...and when one of them meets the other half, the actual half of himself, the pair are lost in an amazement of love and friendship and intimacy and one will not be out of the other's sight even for a moment..."*   Crystal went on to read further.   *"According to Plato's symposium in Greek mythology, humans are originally two of hearts (and two heads, four legs, etc.)   until Zeus began to fear the power of the combined human form, and so cut humans in half, separating them into males and females, resulting into a perpetual ache of separation and longing to regain the completeness by finding one's soulmate."*   Crystal read ahead only to find most of what she was dealing with was matchmaking and dating sites.   But the understanding of term was clearly explained.   As both Roberto and Pauly sat scratching their heads in a state of wonderment and light fog, Crystal took a moment to reflect on the idea as well.   There had been many years in Crystal's past where she thought that she would never have been able to survive a day without Mike's love.   Reading through the internet pages about past lives stirred up a cauldron of forgotten emotions in her.   *Had it not been for Roberto happening into her life and heart when he did, things might have turned out rather lonely and extremely unfortunate for her.   The mystery behind our past-lives and past-loves beholds lifetimes of history only the gifted like Mike and his soul mate, Miranda could begin to understand.* Roberto had assured his loving wife, Crystal that there are predetermined reasons for everything, reasons for great gain, and even great reasons for loss, such as death. Only the great deity with his final design can reveal the truth he intends to teach us all.

Divinity and destiny walk hand in hand as those of us less gifted than those with eternal sight, make an effort to understand the lessons of life where intended experience, time and time again, unfurls anew until the epiphany reveals the awe inspiring outcome and understanding. Crystal was a firm believer in what both Mike and Roberto had been discussing with her in the past. Even Rosemary who played a huge important role as Crystal's mentor, had explained the uncertainties of fate and the grand design. Though many of those non believers chose to follow a design and path of their own, they, eventually, come to find in the end that all routs and alternative ramifications lead to the same final results. Being stubborn and strong willed, Crystal learned the hard way that she could not contest or alter the final outcome. She had come a very long way to discover that her true love and destiny was never too far and always within arms reach the entire time she was searching elsewhere. As the limousine drove closer to her destiny, she thought hard about her path and where it brought her hitherto. *Without resistance being the understanding of destiny and the grand design laid out by the deities, would it not be our falter to seek a cheating cure from fate, by stealing a few more years, and straying from the path?* Crystal's had a dizzying rationale riddled with more questions only a God could answer. *But hasn't God already shown me the answer, plane and obvious?   Truly, it would seem that Jason and his curing gift was handing out complimentary passes that contradicted the rules allowing the privileged to stay on the ride for longer than originally intended.   But was that part of the lesson to be learned?   Do some of us need to struggle harder and longer through the dregs of life more than others?   Are we not equal to learn the same lessons?   Or is it true that some of us retain the innate drive to fight harder and dig deeper, only to feel accomplished, only to feel the right to, finally, possess the rewards we needed to earn on our own to feel worthy and consecrated?*   Crystal fell deep into thought reminiscing her strife and struggle to reach the point in which she had come.   The epiphany Crystal discovered was slow in coming, because her own driven personality could not accept a hand out. To accept an easy break would only rub against grain within her.   She would never allow for a cheat or cut in line.   It wasn't her way.   But now, after looking back on all she represented, it was plane to see, she had earned the right.   She had struggled hard and long for the prize.   And it would stand to reason that it *would* take such an arduous journey to reach the destiny custom designed for her.   Feeling more assured and righteous in her decision, Crystal took the last stand in believing that she had, in fact, earned the right to live.   She deserved to remain the mother of her children and the wife of her doting husband.

While driving across the high desert in a caravan of dutiful soldiers, Crystal's new right of passage was only a few hours away.   And with open arms, she finally surrendered the fight, this one time, to accept her destiny.   Only God himself could have delivered such a gift to her.   Crystal conceded this was the one cheat she couldn't have pulled off on her own.   If the Gods saw fit to hand Crystal a, one time, passage to step to the front of the line and cheat death, Crystal had decided this would be the one time to accept the divine offering with humble gratitude and sincere appreciation.

Now that Roberto and Pauly were totally confused with the logistics of soul mates and twin flames, the ride in the back of the limo hit a lull in conversation as the sounds of the road played a major part in calming everyone's anxieties.

Chapter Seventeen
Unfavorable tidings

Only a few more short miles to their destination, Caroline and El could feel the excitement and anxieties building up from within.   The trip across the nation was a long one, but well worth the prize Caroline longed for.   Though she had told Jack to keep the reception of her arrival quiet and subdued, she prepared for the opposite, expecting to see the excitement of the tickertape party waiting at the threshold of Pauly's estate.   Normally, that's just what Jack would have done.   But upon their arrival, the Calabasas estate was quiet.   The only car in the driveway was Jack's shinny, black Porsche. Caroline pulled up into the driveway along side her husband's car.   Her expectations were disappointed by the absence of dozens of cars parked in every available place, as would be the scene when a party was thrown at the estate.   *Perhaps Jack was taking her request more seriously that she had anticipated,* she thought.

Leaving all the gear and toiletries in the van, except her purse, Caroline exited the vehicle, leading El to the front door with a twinge of glee running thorough her veins.   No sooner she reached to press the doorbell, Jack answered opening the door. Without a single word, Caroline leaped into his arms, nearly pushing him two steps back.   Even El got a kick out of watching her mom act impulsively.

"Wow, it's nice to--"

Locking lips and fully prepared to suck face, Caroline could have successfully played the part of a ravenous, river leach as she relentlessly latched on to her man.   Her jubilant greeting was accepted and graciously returned by Jack's warming embrace. With her feet still inches off the floor, Jack harbored his girl in a bear hug of everlasting devotion. Perhaps such a reception was unexpected from her. Perhaps, she had been too harsh over the phone in the past.   Or could it be, Caroline simply couldn't hide her emotions while in the company of her husband, especially after nearly two years of abstinence.   In either case, Jack was only too happy and excited to see her with such verve and promise.   Though, to El, it might have seemed like an eternity, the twenty second kiss was accompanied by a shower of moans and giggles.

"See you too,"   Caroline finished Jack's thought.   "…my love.   Sorry it took so long to get here, the rental only goes one-hundred twenty-seven miles per hour, at two gallons per mile.   We were forced to make some tedious stops along the way for gas and such…well, okay if you insist, you may have your way with me, now!"   Caroline teased.

"I might try, only…I can't move my arms."   Jack replied, showing a feeble attempt to struggle free from her gripping stronghold.   "Besides, there is a young lady who wishes her turn with daddy."   Jack was already marveling at how big his beautiful daughter had become.

"If you insist."   Caroline said the words, but hadn't yet released her man.

"Caroline…"   Jack reminded, with a smirk of appreciation for her quirky sense of humor.

"Oh, of course."   Caroline reluctantly unwrapped herself from Jack allowing him to have a moment with his daughter.

"Hi, Daddy."   El said, smiling and showing her cute dimples.

"Hi, baby."   Jack said, lifting her up off her feet.   "I sure missed you, sweetie pie."

"I missed you too, Daddy."   Immediately, El began to tear up.   Though she didn't cry aloud, her eyes were quick to pour with streaming tears down both cheeks.   She hugged her daddy around his neck.   No doubt, her daddy could feel her little body giving her all to hang on as tightly as possible.

In the back of Jack's mind he was thinking probably the same as El, '*if only she could continue to hang on so, they might never have to part.*'   "I can't believe how big you've gotten."

No reply came from El, only a tighter hug.

"Well, it's certainly nice to be missed."   Jack reported, looking to Caroline.

"You have no idea…"   She said in reply, trying to appear appetizing, but only managed to pull off a show of a sorrow-filled regret.

"Oh, I might.   I have a fantastic imagination."   Jack smiled, motioning to head to the living room.   "While my appendage and I go to the kitchen, is there anything I can get you?"   Jack asked, already guessing, she would want a tall, glass of sweet, red wine.

"Perhaps a little red wine might be nice." Caroline said with a note of curiosity in her voice. As she looked about the living room and down the hall, clearly, she could see the house was empty. The place was devoid of any sounds at all.   It would be the first time she had ever witnessed the house looking and baring a feeling so desolate.   She knew for a fact that Pauly wasn't home due to her own knowledge and acute deductions.   Never had Pauly been able to handle a quiet house.   In all the times she had visited in the past, Pauly would have every television in the house tuned to different channels. He once explained the constant noise from the televisions and radios kept him from feeling alone. Ever since he lost his wife, he couldn't bare to be alone, it would only remind him of his loss, and cause him stressful sorrows.

With El still strapped to his belly like a little marsupial habitant, Jack returned to the living room with two glasses of Caroline's favorite wine.   "Here we are…"   Jack handed his wife a glass while raising his to propose a toast.

"To penguins and seahorses…"   Caroline beat him to the punch.

"Penguins and seahorses?"   Jack questioned, briefly trying to understand her strange reference.

"Both male species raise their young for a period of time similar to the cute little appendage you wear on your chest as we speak."   Caroline spouted jokingly.

Longingly, Jack looked to Caroline.   "If only I *were* allotted that period of time…"

Perhaps Caroline slipped up by making such a comment involving paternal role-play.   Or maybe it was the subliminal messages coming to surface with the same truth that nagged her every waking hour of every day.   "I know, Jack."   Caroline said solemnly.   "This hasn't been the best arrangement for either of us.   Perhaps, we will get some time later to talk in private."   She remarked, taking a sip of her wine.   A smile came to her lips.   "My favorite.   You are such a sweet man."

"Hopefully, as sweet as your wine."

"Not even close, pal."   She took hold of his hand, sidling closer to him on the couch.   "Nothing can compare to you."   She offered promising messages, only to be doubted by Jack's history of her adamant denials.

"I'm glad to hear that."   Jack said, rubbing Els back with his hand.   "So little monkey, how have *you* been."   Jack redirected his attention to El.

His little daughter released her grip only long enough to answer briefly and take root around his neck once again.   "Been fine."

"And school?   Still getting good grades, I hope?"   Trying to get more than two-word sentences from her, Jack pried on.

"I have been getting all A's.   And my teacher likes me the best."   Proudly, El stated her status.

"Do you think you could sit on the couch next to daddy so he could breathe now, and get a good look at you?"   Jack questioned, using a silly falsetto voice to make his point.

"I guess so, if you insist on breathing."   El said, using one of   her mom's lines as she climbed down from her dad.

"I can see where she gets her sense of humor…"   Jack implied, offering a private sneer to Caroline.

"A chip off the ol' block, I suppose."

Caroline's curiosity finally got the best of her. She just had to know what was up with the empty house.   "So, where is your dad?   You didn't send him away on account of me showing up, did you?" She said, hoping to have been able to see him.

"No actually, it's a bit more complicated than that."   Jack was hedging and listing an esoteric nod toward El.

"How complicated?"   Caroline instantly detected the seriousness of the conversation.

"Very."   Jack hinted, while in the presence of El.   "Perhaps El might want to see the new play room while Mommy and Daddy have a talk."   Jack rose to his feet snatching up his little girl in the process.   "Let's go see what surprises Grandpa Pauly has gathered up for you.   What do ya think?"

El looked to be on the fence with such a hard decision.   Toys have always been the best substitute in times of adult talks.   "Will you stay with me in the playroom?"

"I can, but only for a very short time, sweetie. I need to talk about important stuff with Mommy." Jack lead El down the hall into the playroom that was absolutely amazing, adorned with doll houses and every imaginable Barbie with her inundating accessories.   After Jack set her down, she immediately took hold of a half naked Barbie and stuck her in the pink corvette.   It wasn't long before Caroline joined Jack in the hall.   Coming up behind him, she couldn't resist wrapping her arms around him.   For a few minutes they watched Little El play with the toys, expanding her little imagination, as the dolls took on a life of their own, indulging in conversation and expression.   It was an adorable moment to be sure.   "Okay, little one, Daddy needs to talk for a bit, so I will be back in a few minutes."

        "Uh-huh…"   El's interest had turned to the toys that somehow resembled a torrid orgy of Barbie dolls.

        "I think she likes the new playroom." Caroline commented as they made their way back to the living room.   "So, please, Jack, cut to the chase…what has happened?"   Caroline feared the worst not knowing what to think.   From suspicions of Pauly having a hear attack, to one of the kids falling and breaking a femur or something, every scenario would fleet it's way into her mind while waiting the short time for Jack to return with an answer.

        "It's Crystal.   She is sicker than we first thought."   The look on Jack's face confirmed the seriousness.

        "Oh, God no."   Caroline was already showing signs of dread.   "How sick, Jack?"

        "Final stages of cancer."   Jack didn't see the need in sugar coating the truth.

        "Oh my God, no…"   Caroline broke down. The emotions hit her like a fist to the gut.   Nearly knocking the wind out of her, she tried her best not so be so loud that El might hear her.   "At what hospital is she?   Can we go see her?   Is that where they all are?"

Jack raised a hand to her face, knowing how she can get caught up in one of her rambling thoughts.   With his fingers gently pressed to her soft lips, Jack stopped her amid speech.   "There's a catch, however."   Jack kept his fingers in place keeping her from asking the obvious.   "Dad had found a Shaman that claims Crystal's condition is treatable."   He nodded, already understanding the question she was asking with just her eyes.   "Yes, that is where everyone is already.   However, it is a fairly long drive, nearly ten hours from here.   I thought maybe you would like to shower or eat or something before we leave to go visit her.   It's entirely up to you."   Jack pulled his fingers from her lips.

"How much faith do have in the Shaman?   I have never heard of anyone being able to cure the final stages of cancer."   The mere mention of cancer and the thought of Crystal suffering made her cry even more intensively.

"Dad committed the entire crew to his aid in getting her to the site in Nevada.   He would have taken her anywhere on the planet if he thought he could help to fight the condition.   He must have thought pretty highly of the Shaman to have taken her to see him first, and so far away."

With tears in her eyes and a frog doing her speaking from the throat, Caroline sobbed.   "We should leave right away.   And we should take the van, it's already got all my gear."   Carline slowly began to pull herself together as she thought about the preparation for the trip.   She wiped away the tears, but the redness of her face still remained.   Her sobering staunch could be seen in her eyes.   Jack could tell that she was already putting up her dukes, and getting ready for the brave journey.   This was a side of Caroline he had yet to see.   Like a soldier preparing for battle, Caroline morphed before his very his eyes from a sobbing young woman to a brave foundation of grit and strength.

"That's probably not a bad idea.   I only have a few things packed already if your have the room."

"Plenty of room." Changing the subject, Caroline pressed on with questions.   "Is she suffering?   Was she able to walk on her own?   Did she--?

"This is Crystal we're talking about.   She's like a horse.   She will run and keep   running until the final moment without a whimper or complaint. Quite honestly, after looking at the data Roberto and my dad had shown me before they left here yesterday, I'm convinced Crystal will pull through this favorably.   I know it sounds a bit mysterious, but the proof is in the guys résumé.   He really knows his stuff."   Jack said, trying not to divulge too much information on the matter.   It would seem that the more he might try to explain, the more he feared he would sound crazy and unreasonable.   It was the same reaction he had when Pauly first told him about the Shaman.   But after reading the P. I.'s report, it seemed like the best bet to see Crystal through her illness.   The only analysis Jack might compare the situation to might be that of not only getting the chance to see the legends of aliens and UFO's in person, but also having been given the opportunity to see them in action as they administer the cure for cancer to a family member who just happens to be a saint in the eyes of everyone in the family.   To avoid sounding completely insane, or as Crystal might say, *One nut short of an assortment*," Jack abstained from giving anymore information pertaining to the Shaman.

"I hope you are right, Jack."   Falling back into soldier mode, Caroline remembered the needle of the gas gauge as she pulled into Calabasas.   "We will need to fill the tanks in the van before we head out, and…I'm a bit short on .45 caliber rounds.   I was hoping you could help me out in that department."   Caroline said, hoping to make light of the subject.

Jack smiled warmly.   "Oh, how I love it when you talk guns…so sexy…"   Jack teased as he headed down the hall to get his bags and a few boxes of ammo from the safe.   "you know what they say…happiness is a warm gun…"

"Happiness is feeling protected and secure. I am not advocate of violence, but I wont hesitate to protect my family."   Caroline lessoned as she followed Jack down the hall.   She still harbored some sore feelings about Jack's secret occupation. Making her point, and suggesting her opinion still needed to be aired.

Jack nodded and grinned his answer, "Exactly."   With that, Jack pushed a button on a shelf in the hall.   A picture portrait of a family member popped open just enough to see it had unlatched.   The frame was hinged and made of solid, reinforced steel.   Behind the portrait was a safe operated by a lighted digital keypad.

Caroline examined the craftsmanship of the recessed safe and the efficiency of the workings. With a raised eyebrow she commented,   "Hmmm, very interesting."

"I thought you would appreciate this." Smugly, Jack grinned.

Caroline just shook her head in reply.   She wasn't quite ready to give in to his way of thinking. "Elizabeth…"   Mom called out.   Using her full name was her signal that it was important that she listen.

"Yes, Mommy."   El responded accordingly.

"Daddy has a treat for us.   He has agreed to go on a road trip with us.   Isn't that exciting?" Using her eager voice, Caroline attempted to elevate the mood.

"Aren't you the diplomat."   Jack remarked to his clever wife.

"Cool.   Were are we going?"   El's excitement was refreshing to hear after such a long road-trip already traveled.

"Yeah, well, you definitely don't want to see her dark side."   Caroline warned.

"Oh, I could only imagine where she gets that."   Jack said, implying the obvious as he handed her two boxes of fifty cartridges.

"You just keep your remarks to your self, big fella, and we'll get along just fine."   Caroline retorted.   "Besides, I wouldn't want to reveal where I keep *my* gun."

"Again, I could only imagine."   Jack teased. Changing the subject, Jack turned to El.   "If you would like, and if it's okay with Mom, you are more than welcome to bring some toys along for the trip. It's going to be pretty long, but not as long as the drive you and Mommy already took getting here.

El looked to her mom for approval before scampering back into the playroom to gather some toys.

"Sure, sweetie."   Heading back to the entry way.   Ya know… there was one Barbie I didn't see in there…"

"Is that right?"   Jack questioned, anticipating another of her clever retorts.

"Yea, the new divorced Barbie…she comes with half of Ken's things."

Jack paused a second before making a reply.

Though the joke was humorous, he worried about the implications.   "I hope you're not implying anything by telling me that one."

"Just applying some levity to the room." Caroline noticed that Jack hadn't yet collected his bags for the trip.   "Where's your bags, honey?"

Jack raised his hand and made a fist.   With one gentle, punch strategically placed on a section of the wall in the entry, another hidden panel revealed itself for all to see where Jack had placed his luggage. A locking mechanism had released with a click. What looked like decorative wood molding was actually the sturdy framing of the door for a hidden closet.   Even the ornately carved Sheraton serving table was part of the deception as it was bolted to the hinged door that swung open for Jack to retrieve his luggage.

"Voila."   Said Jack, looking to El who was too busy playing with half naked Barbie and fully naked Ken.   "You see, Mommy's not the only one who hides things behind walls."

El caught a glimpse of the closet door closing back into magical obscurity.   "Do you have food in there, and a phone?"   El was being her systematic and pragmatic self.

Jack wasn't expecting to hear his own lessons thrown back in his face by his own daughter. "Well, no, but now that you mentioned it, grandpa and I will get right one it."   Jack replied almost feeling as though he had just been admonished by his daughter.

"You might want to put some water in there too.   Mommy made a closet with drinks and snacks in it."   El said, as she contorted Ken's arm in every direction except a natural looking one.   She was attempting to pull Ken's arm around Barbie, only she managed to make it look as though he was trying to strangle her with a compound fracture to her throat.

"I guess I better get to work on making better accommodations for our guest who frequent our closet."   As any normal, loving daddy would, Jack surrendered to his little girl's every whim.

"That's okay, just cookies and fruit drinks will be okay, Daddy."   Little El's vocabulary only goes so far at her age.

Jack chuckled, and commented on how well Caroline had raised their daughter.   As he turned to open the front door, Jack realized just how tired Caroline must be from having traveled so far already that day.   "Where are my manners?   Would you like to eat or rest first, or take a shower before we leave?"

"Really, Jack.   Any other time I might have spanked you for being so rude, but I will have to think about it, this time."   Caroline teased.

"I'm not exactly sure how to take that, but I accept."   Jack didn't see the harm in the reciprocation of innuendo.

Just the thoughts that came to mind, made Caroline blush, but only for a fleeting second. Momentary blush was quick to turn to heated emotions with Jack standing so close, and smelling so delicious.   Doing her best to gain back her composure, Caroline quickly remarked,   "I have a terrible feeling this rain check is going to be, painfully, overdue."   Instead of sounding provocative and demurring as she intended, Caroline realized she had just come off sounding more like Maxine and her indiscretions at the club on a Friday night after midnight   (Desperate and horny).

Jack opened the door for the ladies and lead them to the van, after securing the front door of the house.   Looking to the van and getting a better look at its largeness, Jack seemed impressed.   "A bit outspoken, but very nice.”

Caroline pushed the button on the key fob, allowing the side door to slide open for El to jump into the back.

As Daddy helped the little one up the first steep step, he took a gander inside.   “Very impressive.”   Jack nodded.   “Not bad for a rental.”

Caroline knew just where he was leading with another of his lessons.   Beating him to the punch she announced,   “There are one-hundred and sixty-two thousand of these in America alone, and as you might take notice, it has no personal markings whatsoever. The windows are dark tinted all around making it very difficult to clearly identify the occupants inside. And I took the rental number off the license plate frame, making it impossible to detect that it is, in fact, a rental thereby making it virtually impossible to trace it to the registered owner outside of the license plate number like any other vehicle on the road today.   I did my homework.”   Caroline announced proudly and somewhat snobbishly.   After securing El in the back and closing the sliding door, she opened the front passenger door for Jack.   Showing every bit of her independence and her liberated status, she boasted one last announcement.   “I will drive the first shift.”   Caroline looked her man up and down as he climbed inside.   “this is going to be a terribly long drive…”   She mumbled to herself as she shut the d

Chapter Eighteen
Her First Vision

"With the proper foundation of belief, self-determination, love for oneself and others, a positive outlook manifests itself to become a very powerful tool for success with impervious parameters."
Mike Simon

Quite certainly, there was no one more understanding of Crystal's needs and her thoughts than Roberto.   Though Roberto was fully aware of the connection and past between Mike and Crystal, he had no trouble figuring the ramifications that lurked at the back of Crystal's mind.   It would stand to reason that Jason and Crystal must have had a past together, as well.   Twin flame or no, Roberto was clever enough to discern a possible conflict of interest.   Fortunately, Roberto didn't have a jealous bone in his body.   It was never made clear if he and Crystal were soul mates, but that wouldn't stop Roberto from starting anew.   And wherever soul mates are first initiated, in heaven or elsewhere, it didn't matter to either of them.   They had a lifelong pact that they swore to the end.   The loving couple had no doubt that they were made for each other. And though it was a hard and painful lesson to learn, Crystal was taught by Rosemary the very fundamentals of love and paths we take through our journey of many lives.   With timing and sacrifice colliding at intersecting points, every human soul on every living planet will one day have to endure a great loss in love.   It is inevitable.   It is the way of things; the sacrificial way of human growth.   But with Roberto at her side, Crystal believed and understood all her dues and tolls had been paid.   She was no longer thinking about the past with such a bright future as promised.   Fate was becoming her new best friend.   Where she might have scoffed at such notions before, Crystal was stretching her wings to new heights in the spiritual realm.   All the dots were finally being connected in the trials of her life. Rather than contest or resist fate, she learned to take a back seat to the inevitable outcome.   With the research Pauly had conducted, the uncanny connections between lifetimes, and the undeniable past she experienced with Mike and his loving family, it would only stand as fact, her destiny was well planned out.   It was time for her to take confidence that Rosemary was watching over her and assuring the proper outcome of her fateful journey.

The pleasant thoughts of so much abundance in positive energy gave Crystal a warmth of love only her mentor could have delivered accompanied by the familiar fragrance of lilac and rose.   As if she had wrapped her body in the warmth of Rosemary's love, Crystal turned to her side and rested her head on Roberto's shoulder.   Within minutes, she was, quickly, drifting to sleep again.   No doubt, her body was feeling the effects of the disease eating away at her energy level.   And according to the doctors, the pain she was suffering must be excruciating.   No one ever heard her complain.   That was Crystal's way.

Crystal awoke to the noise of thunder blasting a powerful bellow that echoed in her ears.   Feeling the inhibiting effects of having just awakened, Crystal was unable to discern what was happening. Somehow, she had been transported from the car to a strange place she had never seen before.   It was a room, dark and dank with no windows and only one door of entry.   Looming through the darkness, her eyes slow to acclimate, she saw unfamiliar faces standing guard over her.   Next to her, appearing afraid and shaken was her little niece, El.   The thunder that rang through Crystal's ears kept her from understanding what El was trying to say.   As if to be in a panic, El was trying to wake her by shaking her arm and warn her of impending dangers that Crystal was unaware of.   As if to be sluggishly dredging through the quagmire of quick sand, Crystal could neither hear or respond to El's tearful panic. Feeling like she had been drugged, Crystal could only see blurry shadows of foggy impressions moving about her in slow stuttering motion.   With her eyes slowly adjusting to the darkness around her, Crystal could faintly see the attack encroaching into the room she and El were taking refuge in.   The sudden muzzle flash caused temporary blindness to take control over her ability to see.   The explosive report of the rapid gunfire, left a ringing, and painfully deafening impression as well.   The two men keeping vigil over the girls in the small room were the first to be hit by the hail of bullets.   The warm, wetness of blood spatter hitting Crystal in the face required no imagination.   Clearly, the opposition was a rushing force to be reckoned with.   In an instant, the two men who were left to guard and protect the girls had dropped to the ground before getting a shot off.   El let out a bellowing scream as the attackers flooded the room, taking charge.   Looming to view, Crystal could see the men were dressed in dark street clothes and were well armed with fully automatic weapons.

Appearing to be well organized, the attackers hit their intended targets with precision maneuvers.   As they filed into the room after the gunfire had ceased, they took immediate control of the situation.   As though they were military trained, the attacking opposition allowed virtually no time for Crystal to think of an effective defense.   El shrieked and fought valiantly as she was pulled from Crystal's arms.   With little strength in her body, Crystal was no match to the brute force displayed by the number of men that infiltrated the dark bunker.   The combination of the ear-shattering screams coming from El and the commands hollered to the men, had created a befuddling confusion of events for Crystal's wavering mind to follow coherently.   Somehow, she was still unable to move her body to defend herself, much less hold on to El.   Every attempt to move her body was hampered by a lethargic stymie that couldn't be accounted for.   As if her body would only operate in slow sluggish movements, Crystal tried to scratch out the eyes of every man who tried to take hold of her. Unfortunately, her every attempt to defend herself was futile and labored.   As she struggled with the men who held her down, the muscles of her body wouldn't respond properly.   Crystal gave her last attempt to scream out aloud, hoping for a blast of energy to fight off her attackers.   In response to her raucous yell, her face was met with a shattering blow from the butt of a rifle stock.   She was knocked out cold, as El was being taken away by vile strangers.

Sweating and screaming with her palpitating heart fit to burst in her chest and her eyes wide open with a searing blind stare, Crystal lunged up from Roberto's lap in a panic yelling out for Little El's safety.   Roberto and Pauly made every attempt to calm Crystal who obviously had experienced a seriously frightening dream.   They had to physically restrain her to keep from being belted and scratched by her flailing arms and vicious kicks.

Roberto jumped into action attempting to calm her volatile hysterics.   "Crystal, it was just a bad dream, baby.   Everything is okay."   Roberto shouted, trying to be heard over her guttural hollering, and lashing movements.   Even in her weakened condition, her strikes and scratches were to be commended.   Fortunately, Roberto was able to stifle her from causing anyone any serious injury. From within his grasp, he held her tightly and repeated the calming words several times, as she slowly began to adhere to his familiar voice. Without a single tear, she eventually came to her senses, huffing and puffing to catch her breath. Angry fear still festered in her belly as she came around.   Pent up energy was still furiously tracing her pulsating veins.   Every passing second was accounted for with a growing calm.   And even when Crystal knew she was out of danger, she still managed to hang on to the anger and fury that seemed to imprint in her mind.   Once she caught her breath and was able to distinguish the dream from the present, she was able to see clearly and think more sensibly.

"Just a nasty dream, my Bella.   There's nothing that can hurt you."   Roberto continued to coo in her ear as he combed his fingers through her hair, and kissed her forehead.   "You are safe, my love."

"It was El.   They weren't after me.   They got El from me.   I couldn't stop them, Roberto." Crystal felt quite certain that there was some residual truth to her dream.

"Was it a dream or a vision?"   Roberto asked, still fingering her hair, but listening intently.

"I don't know the difference.   I doubt I've never had a vision."   Crystal reported.

"Do you know who they were…the one's who took El?"   Roberto asked, inquiring for specific reasons.

"I didn't recognize them.   It was dark and they were fast…well trained kind of fast."   Crystal said, hedging from her true feelings.

"I've seen that look before."   Roberto made claim.   "Let's have it.   What are you hiding?"

"I'm not even sure really."   Crystal pulled herself up to sit straight in the seat.   As if to better her ability to think, she cracked her neck and stretched her back.   "They could have been anyone, but, somehow, they reminded me of our *own* crew." Crystal was reluctant to admit.

Pauly's ears perked as he too took an interest in her dream.

"It was just a feeling I had.   I can't necessarily make sense of it really…just…a feeling." Crystal said, fading into deep thought.

Roberto looked to Pauly with questioning eyes.

Pauly simply raised an eyebrow, indicating any number of possible scenarios.

"Can you remember what they might have said?"   Roberto questioned, probing for more intel.

Crystal shook her head as she stared off. Her memory of the dream was fading fast. Whatever dialog might have occurred in the dream, was nothing more than a distant and faded past with little hope for any recall.   The only thing that didn't fade from her angry mindset was the fear she heard in Little El's voice as the men grabbed her and carried her off.   The screams from that innocent little girl continued to ring in her ears as her innocence faded away in the distance.

The next two hour's drive in the back of the limo was, for the most part, traveled in gestating silence.   It had seemed that each one of them were trying to make sense of the dream as they concentrated in solitary thought.   Pauly made a call to one of the crew, suggesting a few instructions. Though he was only working on a hunch, Pauly wasn't one to gamble or ignore a vision.   In his mind, Crystal wasn't one to exaggerate or mince words.   Whether it was a dream or a vision, Pauly wasn't willing to take any chances.   He sent for a crew to return to the estate to meet up with Jack and his family.   With nearly all the main crew members already out in force, Pauly had to call upon some of the reserve force for back up.   Little did Pauly realize, that turned out to be his biggest, most regrettable, mistake.   Unbeknown to anyone, a vicious vendetta was brewing in the mix.

Chapter Nineteen
Crystal's arrival

*"I promise you nothing because tomorrow does not
yet exist.
I give you today what I would every day.
But so far, now is only a moment of our today.
Your dreams will fulfill with every waking moment.
Tomorrow's promises are victims of circumstances.
Remember that tomorrow is never what it is imagined
to be today."   Samantha Shane*

At the halfway point of the drive out to the
Indian reservation in Nevada, the entire convoy made
a stop to fuel up and for restroom needs.   Lumbering
out of the Limo was first lead by Pauly.   Once
several of the crew members from the other cars
came to his aid, he was lead to the restroom.   He
had a bit of limp to his walk when he first stretched
his feet.   It wasn't the ride that had cramped his
style, nor was it his circulation that was hampered by
the drive.   What went unannounced was the fact that
when Crystal had been kicking and struggling to get
free from her captures of her dream, Pauly had
inadvertently sustained a painful kick to the testicles.
Fortunately, he didn't suffer any permanent damage,
nor was he planning on having anymore children.
And no one had the tenacity to mention his strange
gate.

A second set of men came to aid with Crystal
and Roberto.   As they escorted her to the ladies
room, a young girl who had just exited the restroom,

immediately recognized her as the famous pop singer.   The young girl looked to be in total amazement, as if to think that famous people don't have the need to urinate.   Upon requesting an autograph, the young girl didn't seem to be intimidated by all the body guards standing in formation around Crystal.   Without hesitation, Crystal felt obliged to fulfill the girl's request.   After all, Crystal thought, it's not everyday an ex-pop star gets recognized, especially without her make-up.   The young girl riffled through her purse, and was, finally, able to find an old shopping receipt.   Gleefully, she handed the narrow slip of paper to Crystal who accepted it graciously.

"What's your name, sweetie?"   Crystal asked as she turned the girl around so to use her back as a writing board.

"My name is Crystal.   My mom named me after you."   The young girl proudly announced.   "She has all your music."

The age reference suddenly kicked Crystal in the gut.   Roberto bit his lip, attempting not to chuckle aloud, as he realized Crystal hadn't expected to hear such a guileless answer.   *'To Crystal and her mom, best wishes and perhaps we may meet in pee once again.'*   Was what she wrote on the receipt before handing the young girl the paper and entering the restroom.   No doubt, Crystal was humbly beginning to feel her age.

Once the entire convoy was back on the road again, Roberto apologized to Crystal for finding the young girl's comment humorous.   "I owe you an apology for slipping up back there.   I think she caught us both by surprise."   He announced, genially offering his apology.

"I thought I heard you snickering."   She

said, grinning in a way that only Crystal could do and still look deadly serious.   "You have nothing to apologize for, baby.   We're getting older, my old man.   And if I could look half as beautiful as Rose did at her age, I would gladly sign dozens of autographs for the grandmother's fan club.

Roberto could be heard sighing aloud. "You will always be beautiful, my Bella."

"I will try to remember that when you sign me up for the geriatrics glee club."

Roberto laughed in reply, loving how clever her mind worked.

The convoy made two more stops through the night travels.   Along the way, Roberto and Crystal talked about the esoteric properties of Jason's gift and who he chooses to use it for.   With Pauly sound asleep, Roberto was able to talk frankly.   Though Roberto didn't know the exact amount of money paid forward for her treatment, all three boys had chipped in with Pauly paying out the largest percentage.   He insisted on making sure all of Jason's needs were met, including security and transportation to the reservation.   Crystal could not have been more grateful for the love and support of her family.   She was loved by everyone, and Pauly wanted to assure her, he would do everything possible to make her life comfortable.   The mood remained melancholy as the couple talked over nearly every topic.   They spoke of her advanced directive, and her will. Making sure no stone went unturned, they covered all aspects of what might come of her condition.   It was a sobering conversation, to say the least. Fortunately, they both held on to hope.   When Mike Shane's daughter, Samantha wrote a book called *'Philosophy The Obsession,'*   She had dedicated a significant page that Crystal held dear and close to her heart.   It was called, 'The Soul.'

"The soul.   We generally refer to our inner self as the soul.   The dictionary describes our soul as a **nonphysical aspect of person:** the complex of human attributes that manifests as consciousness, thought, feeling, and will, regarded as distinct from the physical body.

Distinct from the physical body...even the dictionary claims a separation between body and soul.   Scientists have already documented a body that had just died was suddenly twenty-one grams lighter the moment death occurred.   This proven fact has been studied and witnessed more than once. This study dates back to 1907.   The calculations were correct every time, and all instrument calibrations were conducted before and after the experiment.

So I ask you, where did the soul go?   Do you doubt the scientific tests to be valid?   Do you believe the soul simply floated away into oblivion never to been heard from again?   Do souls float into space to become something we know nothing about? Do souls become our guardian angels?   Do they simply roam the Earth aimlessly?   If they remain Earthbound, are they aware of us?   Do you believe in reincarnation?   Do you believe in ghosts, spirits, poltergeists or haunting?   If so, do you suppose the soul returns to a new body sometime in the future. How many souls do think there might be? According to some, the guff is a limited number of souls waiting to experience life in the physical form. And once the guff is depleted mankind will have reached his time; time for the apocalypse.

Some claim death is final, no returns, no passing GO and collecting $200.00, no experiences to recall and no existence whatsoever, here or *anywhere, forever.   The concept of finality to non-existence from corporeal form, to me, is less acceptable than any pain I have yet to experience.*

Many people who have had near death experiences (NDE) claim that they saw a bright light while feeling pulled to a destination.   They also claimed that the pain and suffering that plagued them in life had not only vanished, but their state of mind and psyche had completely transformed to a halcyon calm that they vaguely remember feeling, but not from a time when they were alive.   Others who have had NDE say they had felt not only the absence of pain, but a sense of nirvana so strong that they actually regretted coming back when revived. Others who were able to recollect their NDE after being revived wanted nothing more than to return to what they considered to be home, a higher, sacred place.   Could it have been heaven?   Does that mean there is a Hell?   Does that confirm there is a God?

My NDE was somewhat different from these said accounts.   My death was not a painful one.   I suffer from a heart disorder.   My disorder is congenital.   When my first death experience came I was fully aware of my predicament.   (I omit the word near because I was clinically dead just like so many others.)   I don't believe there is anything nearer to death than death itself.   Like many others, who might have been revived, but had we not been, death was certain.

My death was slow to occur.   I was passively falling into a sleep stasis as my heart simply stopped functioning properly.   There was some discomfort, nothing compared to so many other's NDE.   My fondest memory of death was the nirvana.   I felt it immediately.   I concur with others who felt

*disappointed to be revived.   Though I am fond of life
and chose to be alive, I can see how many would
choose otherwise.   If this nirvana were to come in a
pill form, I doubt anyone would be able to keep from
becoming a junkie once tried and experienced.
Aside from the wondrous calm of elated spirits and
the dearth of discomfort, I recall very little else.
Perhaps time is relevant when dead.   Maybe I
wasn't dead long enough to know what more was to
come.   It took the paramedics around three minutes
to revive me from the grasp of my demise.
I have spoken with many who claim to have
experienced the nirvana.   Each one of them claim
that they have never again felt anything close.*

 *In my case, I have felt it on many occasions
while still alive.   I don't know what brought it on.
I don't know if or when it will ever happen again.
But I do know, the feeling is like nothing I could
possibly explain with words.   I had once fallen to my
knees with pleasure permeating my body and mind.
It was like suddenly being overdosed by an explosion
of endorphins.   Both physical and mental sensors
were misfiring all at once.   Not that any of this
would necessarily be a bad experience, however,
imagine (as best you can) having an orgasm, falling
in love and winning the lottery all at once.   The
sensory overload of such an event would not be my
concern…to the contrary, it would be the recovery
from such an experience that worries me.   I still
remember how it made me feel, each time, exactly the
same and just as powerful.   How does one recover
from this without wanting to go back?   Do I invite
death?   Absolutely not.   Because of my heart
condition, I know I have a purpose and a foreseeable
journey that has yet to be fulfilled.   I believe I have
a mission to complete by helping others who suffer
from a terminal illness as I do.   But I can say*

*without reservation, I do not fear death.   However, I
do not live fearlessly absent of caution.   I simply live
each day to the fullest, but not as though it were my
last, of course…I do have a retirement plan.
For those who face the terminal inevitability, I say
don't fear it.   Know there is love beyond the stars."*
Samantha Shane

Chapter Twenty
The will to live.

The Will

"If I was given a voice, I would sing you an enchanting heart throbbing, mind tantalizing love song.
If I was given muscles, I would embrace you and show you warmth within my fortress.
If I were given rhyme, I would write you enticingly beautiful poetry.
If I was made hypnotic, I would capture your attention and keep you eternally regaled.
If I was given speed, I would appear before us all, and offer my all.
If I was given love, I would prove myself contagious.
If I was given remedy, I would heal all.
If I was given humor, your tears would be that of joy.
If I was given legs, I would teach you to dance.
If I was given a mind, I would calculate reason and time.
If I knew about happiness, I would void sad.
If I was given more existence, I would be.
If I was given the ability to trust, we would all be free.
But instead of all this, I was given the will.   The will to do as I please.   The will to live.   The will to prove myself able.   The will to make it all plausible which makes it all possible and fulfilled."
Samantha Shane

The arrival at the Indian reservation was none too soon.   Crystal was feeling the aches and discomfort of the long miles.   Not knowing what to expect to see at a reservation, she looked forward to the sights.   However, upon first impression, she couldn't help but feel a strong sense of depravation and decadence.   After passing through the front gate of the reservation, a young man in his pickup truck had stopped the convoy momentarily.   The marking on his truck read, *'Tribal Police Indian Affairs.'*   He introduced himself as Johnny Whitefeather.   He had been expecting the visit, and proceeded to lead the convoy deep into town.   The level of poverty that Roberto and Crystal witnessed from the tinted glass of the shinny limousine was far below anything she might have guessed it to be.   *The question that struck her was why stay and continue to live in such desolation if it is so inhibiting?   Were they prisoners, not permitted to leave?   Is this all our government allots them to survive with?   Could this be how they choose to live?*   Far be it for her to judge, but Crystal could not imagine how anyone would choose to live in such poverty.   Some natives were actually residing in nothing more than fifteen foot long travel trailers with no windows, electricity or fresh running water.   The conditions seemed deplorable.   As they drove deeper into town, Crystal tried to gain a sense of understanding, but to no avail did any of it make sense to her.   She witnessed people asleep on front porches.   Some were neglected of any shelter at all, sleeping on benches by the tiny local store.   Some residence looked no better off than the feral dogs that rummaged through the tipped trashcans scrounging for scraps.

        Roberto could sense the growing anger welling up inside Crystal.   It was her immediate impression that the American government was responsible for the poor living conditions inflicted upon the native people.   Though no history books in the American school system every speak of the treaties or the agreements made between the American Indians and the settlers, Crystal was already convinced of the federal involvement of such neglect and unfair treatment.   In the world of politics, and bureaucratic hypocrisy, innocent people caught in between will, no doubt, suffer the most. Though Crystal was appalled by what she was seeing, she stifled her emotions and tried to concentrate on the matter at hand.   She was nervous and riddled with anxieties.   She didn't know whether to allow her hopes to rise, or simply take it with a grain of salt.   As the limo pulled up to a small house off of a quiet dirt road, they were met with several other cars of the Tribal Police.   Pauly's crew was quick to pull their vehicles around to secure the area as they parked in protective formation strategically around the house forming a blockade of cars and trucks. With several of the limousines appearing identical, there was no way of detecting which car housed the family of interest should an attack breakout.   At the last of the positioning of the cars, many of Pauly's crew gathered at the proper vehicle.   Each of his men were sporting automatic firearms as they assembled to protect the family and their trek into the little house at the end of a dusty, dirt path. Inasmuch as Crystal was weak and tired by this time, two gunman were chosen to help guide her into the house.   With both her arms around the guy's necks, she was lifted up off her feet and carried the full distance.   At the door, they were met by a young woman who introduced herself as Sara.   She had long, black hair that shined with the refection of the sun.   As a light breeze caught her hair, it looked to be straight and flowing like water ripples.   She was a young woman who carried herself proudly.   As she opened the screen door wide for Crystal and the two boys to enter, the rest of the crew stood standby outside the door and around the entire house.   Once inside, Crystal was placed on a couch.   As soon as she was safely secured, the two gunman returned to their post outside and stood guard by the door.   Two of Pauly's men were already inside the house standing at the ready.

  Sara was the first to initiate the introductions.

The house was small and there was little seating for everyone inside.   Sara pointed out her boy friend and introduced him first.   Her boyfriend was called White Horse, as he refused to use his given name of Terrance.   Standing next to the dinning room table was Jason Mathison, the man of the hour.   Jason, first shook hands with the gentlemen of the room before conducting himself with Crystal. Immediately, Jason gave off an aura of warmth and kindness.   He was absent of ego or any notions of grandeur.   His friendly nature was easily accepted as he approached Crystal and began to talk freely and explain the procedure.

"It's truly a pleasure meeting with you, Crystal.   I have to admit, I was a bit nervous meeting you.   And by the way, you have a lot of good friends in very high places."   Jason announced reaching to shake her hand.

"I think the pleasure is, more so, mine.   Until the other day, I had never heard of you, then I came to find that you are, somehow, intertwined with everyone I know and have loved."   Crystal said, shaking his hand.

"Strangely, it does seem to work that way a lot of the time.   Perhaps after the treatment, at a more convenient time, we could all get together and investigate our family tree.   I am betting there is more to it than we realized, even today."   Jason smiled with confidence and a note of privy information.   But his motions seemed rushed and slightly uneasy.   He wasn't admitting it, but he was hiding something.

"I could only imagine…"   Crystal said.

Moving quickly, Jason assembled some medical utensils on a tray.   "I am sorry to have to rush things along, however, I will explain why when we finish with the procedure."   Jason assembled a syringe and some fresh alcohol swabs.   "This is a relatively easy procedure for the both of us, Crystal. All I do is withdraw some blood from my arm, and it gets injected into you."   Jason didn't need to see the look that Crystal was already casting some doubt and trepidation.   "Yes, I am sure you are thinking that it sounds quite primitive and unorthodox, however, I have done this more that a thousand times, and have never lost a single patient.   I couldn't begin to explain the finer details of how this all works exactly because, unfortunately, we don't have weeks to discuss it.   The history of this process goes back as far as the Mayans.   Thankfully, the government hasn't gotten their hands on all of us who carry the gene to cure."   After inserting the needle into his own his own arm, Jason drew blood from a vein just as he first described.   As he approached Crystal, he couldn't help but notice just how beautiful she was in person.   Her brown eyes seemed to loom up at him with innocence and a lifetime of stories.   "Are you ready?"   He asked, opening a alcohol swab package. The smell of alcohol filled the room with it's strong medicinal odor.

"As I will ever be, I guess."   Crystal replied, taking a deep breath and nodding her head as she looked to her husband for support.

Jason swabbed her arm and followed up with the syringe filled with blood.   "Take a breath, old soul and friend, for today is your lucky day."   Said Jason, taking hold of her arm and gently pressing the needle to her flesh.   On the count of three, the procedure was done and the needle was withdrawn. Okay, young lady, I have seen the positive results in as little as three hours, and as long as three days before the full effect might take place.   So, my suggestion to you is, simple; rest here on the couch and wait for the miracle to take place.   I assure you,

you *will* be pleased."   Jason turned and gave a nod to Roberto and Pauly, motioning to follow him outside.

"We will be back in a bit, Babe."   Roberto told Crystal as he stepped out of the front door with Jason and his dad.   Neither of them had any idea what Jason had on his mind that was very concerning.   Something seemed pressing and important to Jason as they gathered outside to have a word.   Hoping it didn't have anything to do with Crystal's condition, both boys were anxious to know what had urged Jason to lead them outside for such an important discussion.   Little did the boys know, the subject matter at hand had nothing to do with Crystal, but had everything to do with the safety of Jack, Caroline and El.

Chapter Twenty-one
The Reckoning

"In a time before internet, before instant

Jack and the girls set out on the road together for the first time in over a year.   Though the circumstances of Crystal's illness was an ominous black cloud darkening their excitement, the three of them made the best of the travel arrangements just the same.   Without going into too much detail, Caroline told El that Aunt Crystal was sick.   She didn't explain the severity or the extent of her condition.   If all was to go well, Caroline wouldn't need to discuss any of the details again.   As far as El knew, they were merely traveling to visit with Crystal in a special hospital.   Truth be told, if Jason's miracle blood was to fail, the trip to Nevada would, probably be the last time anyone would be seeing her. With her condition deteriorating as fast as it was, there would be no hope of her making it back to the estate in Calabasas.

As Caroline drove the first leg of the trip, she did her best to keep a positive frame of mind.   She had never before heard of things such as, Shamans and medicine men except from what she might have seen in the Hollywood movies.   She had little confidence in such hopes as they epitomized the fable side of reality.   Caroline was a realist.   She didn't believe in magic or miracles.   And she had little use for fate.   Crystal was a good soul, that Caroline knew and understood to be true.   But surrendering to the hand of fate wasn't to Caroline's liking.   She believed too many good people in her life had died. Too many young children are suffering from terminal illnesses everyday.   How could fate account for so many losses, and still hold any validity?   It didn't make sense to her, nevertheless, one redeeming factor did remain in her regimen of survival.   She had always believed that God was in control, and God could make the changes if he saw fit.   So Caroline would pray.   Her one redeeming trait held in high regard by the spirits that watch over us all, was her guardian angel who always listened to her prayers.

"Love is hope with an open heart.   And prayer is an open heart sought to replenish your soul. Without hope you are a lost soul absent of love."
Mike Simon

Instead of making due with the rations that were supplied in the back of the van, Jack had suggested El pick out her favorite fast food.   Before El uttered a word from her mouth, Caroline was already doing her best to keep from laughing aloud. Knowing her daughter quite well, the answer was no secret.   But the etiquette behind the answer might have been a bit surprising to the novice father who wasn't familiar with El's vernacular.
"I think I would like to eat at McDonalds." Little El announced, already salivating from the thought of the savory honey mustard sauce.
"Sounds good to me."   Daddy answered. "And what does Little El generally eat at McDonalds?"
"The usual, chicken boobies with honey mustard sauce."   El answered, matter-of-fact.
After Mom and Dad had a good laugh, they, simultaneously, felt the familiar pang of a flaming heart throb that had long been smoldering unattended.   They exchanged looks of promise and sultry thoughts.   "Chicken boobies it is…"   Jack fondly announced, taking a liking to the newly coined food product.   As they continued to drive to the fast

food restaurant, Jack and Caroline had continued to experience a privy moment, racing their hearts and causing naughty thoughts.   Rolling eyes, deep respiring breaths and biting lips were all that could suffice.   It would be hours, maybe days, before Jack and Caroline would get a chance to share any private time together.   The anticipation was building in up both of them.   Had El not been in the van, the two of them might have jumped each other three-times-over already.   Jack was certain that he wasn't receiving mixed signals which made the long trip all the more invigorating and filled with anticipation.   Caroline could see his mind was traveling at a million miles per hour, just dying to tear her clothes away, and strap her to the bench seat in the back of the van. Of course, that was wishful thinking on her part, no doubt.   Aside from the familiar messaging grins, Caroline could only read that he was more than willing to rekindle their marriage at the drop of a hat. The thoughts of torrid sex acts were her doing, or in her case, *her undoing*.

     After stopping off at the fast food place, they were back on the road heading north into the night. It wasn't long after leaving the restaurant, Jack got a call from one of Pauly's standby crews requesting his location.   After a brief conversation and a quick look at the map, Jack gave the information and informed the crew of where they might meet.   The added security gave both Jack and Caroline a good feeling of family unity that Caroline had been yearning for and missing for quite some time.   After a slight change in direction heading East on the Interstate 15 instead of taking the coast on the 101, a new rout was figured in so both teams could meet up somewhere in Los Vegas Nevada.   Though Jack was planning on driving through the night all the way to their destination, the plans would have to change just

slightly in order to join up with the other team.
They would need to stop for a short time allowing the
other crew to catch up.   Already, Caroline's mind
was fast at work arranging the beds in the back and
fantasizing the consummation of her reunion with
Jack.   If ever fate was to play a role in Caroline's
sexual affairs with her husband, this had to be the
perfect timing of fateful romance.   Pushing the
speed limit and cutting every corner along the way,
Caroline did her best to make way to the place that
Jack had circled on the map.   It was a camping
outfit that catered to motor home sales, parts and
service.   It was the perfect spot to park and blend in
with the other campers and vans while waiting.
According to Jacks figures, he calculated they would
be in Los Vegas in in just a little over two hours.   Or
one and a half hours if Caroline was to drive at one-
hundred twenty seven miles per hour.   If she had her
way, she would have tried.

        The next two hours were the worst Caroline
had traveled all week.   She was nearly crawling out
of her skin to get at Jack.   She cursed the rental van
for being governed at seventy mile per hour.   No
matter how hard she pushed that accelerator, it
refused to travel any faster than seventy.   When El
decided to lay down in the back, she was fast asleep
as soon as her head hit the pillow.   But before she
went to bed, she made sure to kiss her daddy good
night, and tell him how much she enjoyed having him
stay with them.   It was a touching moment, to say
the least.   That little girl knew exactly how to pull
those heartstrings.   Of course, fact remained, El
loved her daddy and missed him very much.   There
was no denying the separation of family was
detrimental for all of them involved.   Once El was
fast asleep, the conversation turned from G rating to
R real fast.   Jack teased and enjoyed watching

Carline squirm in her seat.

"You need to stop doing that.   You're getting me…"

"I'm sorry, I didn't hear that last part.   What was it you said?   You're getting what?"   Jack asked as obnoxiously as possible.   "Did you say wet?"   Jack reached over the center consol to her upper thigh at the most ticklish part.   All it took was one tiny squeeze, and Caroline was giggling uncontrollably.   The van began to swerve slightly as Caroline was quick to regain control.

"Hey!   You trying to get us all killed?" Caroline played along, trying desperately to contain herself.

"Hardly."   Jack was quick to retort.   "I was just attempting to get that leg of yours to push the accelerator a tad harder."

"Oh yeah, that's all we need…a speeding ticket in the middle of the desert.   And how do you explain all these guns crossing the border, cowboy?" Caroline was just as much in a rush as he, although the consequences would have been far too great to bear.   "Not that I don't want your hands all over me, I just want to get there in one piece."   Caroline claimed as she was nearly panting with an excessive amount of unspent sexual energy.   Her squirming in the driver's seat was becoming a force of habit. "Besides, this would probably be a bad location to be found parked on the side of the road, butt-naked and wildly involved in an inseparable sex act that only a billion PSI fireman's hose could extinguish.   And to be quite honest with you, I don't think a billion PSI would be effective about now."

"Well, as long as we are being honest with each other, I guess this is as good a time as any to tell you I have been missing you, big time, sweet girl." Jack said, being as humble as possible.

"Oh, babe…that's really not helping matters right now."   Frowned Caroline, indulging heavily in his sincerity.

"Can't help it, honey.   It's the truth.   At some point we will need to sit down talk about this…about us."   A sobering tone of seriousness overtook the mood.

"I know.   You are right."   Caroline confessed as the sexual tension began to taper off, but not completely.   "We will have that talk, I promise you."

Jack's eyes denoted a sign of gratefulness. In his mind, he never got that chance to explain himself.   He was never allowed his due process. Caroline had witnessed the very dregs of his business and drew upon her own conclusions without so much as allowing Jack his explanation before impetuously leaving.   Without so much as a note, Caroline was packed and out of Jack's life for good before his work day was, halfway, complete.   No doubt, what Caroline saw on that fateful day was the most horrible, cold blooded murder scene she could have imagined.   But the fact remains, she didn't hear his side of the story.   She didn't stop for a moment to consider there might have been an explanation. From the moment her eyes saw innocent children slain where they stood, and a nefarious drape of ugliness drew upon a indelible, nightmarish outcome. With red flags waving and maternal instincts on high alert, Caroline did what any protective mother would do.   By separating her child from any possibility of danger, she did her best to preserve the sanctity and preservation of the life of herself and child.   And she did so, in that order.   One very important fact she learned from Jack was the order in which to rank preservation.

In studies conducted by both the sheriff

department and the police department, it had been apparent that in ninety-five percent of car jacking cases and kidnapping cases, the parent that kept a level head at the time of abduction was the parent that lived to see another day with their child.   The study of abduction, each time, revealed fact and truth that the parent who fought the abductors at the time of abduction were the ones who lost their lives, never to see the outcome of their child's safety.   Though it is, by far, the most difficult thing to do, the parent must take into account and understand the futility of a situation without escalating the outcome of dangers and even death.   As Jack had lessoned Caroline before, the history of kidnapping cases had proven beyond a doubt that the only way to guarantee the safety of the child is to make certain that you, the parent, stay alive to see another day.   Those that did not take heed to such understanding, fought a worthy battle only to lose the war and everything vitally important in the end.   That ninety-five percent that fought against the odds to save their child's life at first impulse, lost everything left to bargain with. And those that recognized the imminent dangers yoked with the preservation of life were fortunate enough to have lived to see their child safe and healthy another day.   The day Jack had taken the time to explain such studies, Caroline had a very hard time dealing with the idea of allowing a kidnapper to take her child from her.   Even at gunpoint, she knew her own instincts would have been to fight the attackers.   Most people who have children of their own, or have been given custody, permanent or temporary, will act and feel the same way.   Jack further explained that it is our nature as protectors and parents to oppose those who impose a threat especially against our children and family members. But it is the one, *and only the one* who can maintain a steady mind and keep control of the situation by not panicking, by not escalating the dangers, that will come out ahead.   As Caroline understood the lesson thoroughly, she had yet to know how she would actually react in such horrific circumstances. As all of Jack's lessons had eventually come to fruition, Caroline had done her best to take into account every possibility of opposition.   She prided herself with her marksmanship and abilities with guns, as she had also taken a few self-protection classes.   She studied at length the unforeseen probabilities of every attack she might encounter.   After her fight with the gang bangers and the attempted rape, she had learned a great deal more, and taken into account more ways to improve her chances of survival.   Her firsthand lessons were as vital as training and guidance tools. However, Caroline was fully aware that not every possible attack can be accounted for.   There will always be an unforeseen angle that was never thought of or reasoned with.   All one could do is try to expect the unexpected and work with your skills while keeping a level head.   Sometimes, quick, lightning reflexes, are not the proper reactions to danger.   And, especially, when it comes to our children, no one can prognosticate just how we might react.

Chapter Twenty-two
The Challenge of Instincts

Traveling to the next destination to wait for backup, was a long two hour drive, but well worth their arrival.   El was fast asleep in middle partition of the van, just behind the driver's seat.   The larger, more secluded area at the back of the van had a private accordion door with magnetic latching devices.   The accommodations were well worth the accolades from parents with children on long trips or simply camping out.   The only other hindrance might have been the fact there was no sound proofing.   And Caroline tends to be loud in certain carnal situations.

Upon arriving at the meeting place at the outskirts of Las Vegas Nevada,   Caroline exercised her habitual routine of defensive actions.   She strategically surveyed the entire rest stop before deciding upon the most suitable place to park the van. She took every possible scenario into account as she made her finally decided where to park and make camp.

Jack's eyes and smile were a token of his appreciation for her, well learned expertise.   He needn't say a word to aid in their safety; he didn't have to.   His protégé had exceeded his teachings. He was further impressed with the electronic devices that she set up and activated upon parking the van. Like a well greased machine, Caroline moved about the inside of the van, activating all the proper security measures.   As Jack sat back and watched her work, he couldn't help but feel proud to know his daughter and wife were well protected and taken care of when he wasn't present.   None of Jack's crew knew the extent of her skills.   The only evidence of her survival techniques were the bodies of bad guys she had left behind in her wake.   Watching firsthand, the art of her work was confirmation of good training and study.   He certainly was proud of his wife. Though it was never her intention to be one of the crew, she was well on her way to becoming a well trained soldier of war.   Where most passive people of the world choose not to look or believe unprovoked violence occurs each day, Caroline had experienced the contrary evidence that divides the meek from the warrior.

Caroline took just a few minutes to set up her procedural routine, and make up the bed for her and Jack.   All the while, she did her best to keep her mind on her business and not Jack's body.   But the effort was challenging, to say the least.   She attempted to keep herself centered until the chores of security were completed.   The camera was in place and activated.   The monitor and such were powered up and drapes were drawn for privacy.   All that remained was to strip off her clothes and mercilessly throw herself at her husband.   To wait another minute might have caused a shameless, spontaneous compulsion to rape him…violently.   Without a second to waste, after Caroline set the monitor in the same place as she had done so previously, she invited Jack to join in her in the back.   The sexual tension was like heated water just about to boil.   After turning on the console radio in the back to help cover up some of the potential sounds, she sat Jack on the edge of the bed, and closed the folding partition.   As the magnets pulled to a click, the door was secured and Caroline moved accordingly.   Facing her man, she wasted no time in removing her shirt.   Her lacy bra was one she had especially picked out just for the occasion.   She watched his eyes widen and his pupils dilate as he observed her fleshy, white skin become exposed for his pleasure.   The emitting light of the monitor allowed for just enough luminance to see all the action that was about to unfurl.   As the cashmere sweater hit the floor of the van without a sound, Caroline reached to the back of Jacks head, running her tender fingers through his, slicked-back, hair, she guided his lips to her soft belly.   Her entire body tingled as he landed a gentile kiss on her waiting flesh.   The bumps of pleasure permeated throughout the surface of her naked skin.   His hands reflexively reached up to take hold of her, hourglass, shaped hips.   His first kiss lead to two, then three, and God knows how many more after that.   He squeezed and kneaded her fleshing skin with his masculine fingers.   From her midsection to the material of her sexy little bra, Jack traced a trail of tender kisses that drove shivers up her spine…and other places too.   His deft hands were quick to move upon their own accord on up to her waiting breasts. His titillating touch worked wonders at her nipples, hardening them like small pebbles.   The thin material of the lacy bra left nothing to the imagination, especially, with her rock-hard nipples protruding like steadfast missiles poised for launch. Every advancement of his hands and stealthy fingers lead to more panting breaths and inaudible whimpers she couldn't have controlled if her life depended on it.   Harder, she pulled at the back of his head causing him to place his kisses upon her breasts.   In reflexive response, his lips pressed ever so gently against her cleavage and up to her neck.   Without warning, Jack had pulled her bra upwards allowing her supple breasts to fall free and exposed fully.   His kisses trailed downwards from the tenderness of her neck back to her cleavage.   As his hand assisted by pressing her breasts together, he continued to kiss each of her firm boobs individually.   Using his slightly, parted lips, he traced a rout of loving

caresses over every surface of her breasts, save that
of her erect nipples.   Saving them for later, he
parted his lips allowing his tongue to leave a trail of
glistening saliva over her sweetened, soft flesh.
Before she knew he had made the effort, her bra was
unclasped and falling to the floor along side her top.
The pure nakedness of her upper body had equal
effect on both of them, raging their heart rate and the
euphoric arousal to a steamy shower of emotions.
Caroline responded diligently to his every call.
With his fingers squeezing and caressing flesh, she
was losing control over demurring patience.   Her
fingers were now grasping and pulling at his hair
with every intent to imbibe every afforded pleasure
he so freely delivered unselfishly and expertly.   Her
moans escalated to pitchy whimpers and gasps of
audible pleasure.   Jack moved with methodical
precision, knowing exactly what his wife craved and
responded to best.   Knowing just how sensitive her
sweet nipples were, he made every effort to stay clear
of touching them, coming within microns of them
with his iterant tongue.   As Caroline fell quicker
into the spell of the moment, Jack had already
unbuttoned and removed his shirt.   He raised to his
feet nearly touching the roof of the van with his head.
Flesh against naked flesh, Jack reeled her close and
planted a passionate kiss upon her slightly parted lips.
She was so caught up in his play, she hadn't yet
noticed how things were already progressing.   She
received his kiss with overwhelming wanton, nearly
colliding teeth as she responded vigorously.   The
passion of such a deep kiss could have had volumes
of books written about it.   Every imaginable feeling
of passion streamed its way through both their
bodies, climbing to summits of rampant, neck-
writhing.   As if to of been rehearsed to the timing of
perfection, the two of them, simultaneously,

separated just long enough to strip themselves free of all their clothes.   The synchronized movements were undeniably perfected by many nights of similar practices of their past.   They knew and understood each other quite well.   On every level, they were mates of a thousand lifetimes.   Reunited, and completely naked, and free to resume the ravaging, they came together with another engaging kiss of deep passion and surrendering moans from the both of them.   Like the melding of heated liquid in a lava lamp, their hands and bodies seemed to move and fold into each other.   Conjoined in the other's stronghold, they remained pressed firmly against the fleshy nakedness of the other.   The sensation of nothing hindering lead to a heated progression of kisses from Jack on down her neck and back to her waiting breasts.   Spending only enough time to drive her crazy with anticipation, Jack continued on down with kisses to her belly and lower area beneath her navel.   He slowing sat himself back on the edge of the bed never losing cadence with his trail of tender kisses.   He knew exactly what worked best to drive her to the point of harmonic ecstasy.   Like a finely tuned pitchfork, Jack worked to tune his art upon her sexy naked body.   In response, her resonation vibrations could be felt and heard in every response she did emit.   His kisses finally made way to the pleasure zone of her ultimate desires.   At the very instant her legs gave way to euphoric spells, Jack took hold of her body, showing little effort, lifted her up off her feet, he pivoted around on one foot.   Switching places, he placed her on the bed and dropped to his knees in front of her.   Every orchestrated movement was conducted by Jack's torrid desire to ravage his woman with oral justification and satisfaction.   Like a starved wolf, Jack took her, feasting on her wetness.   Spreading her legs to the limit, he pulled her closer to the edge of the bed, all the while his lips planted tender loving kisses around her privates.   Taking in her scent and flavor, Jack spent little time circling his prey, before the final dive to the center of his attraction.   His kisses lead to long, savory wet spots at every stop. With his warming tongue adding more wetness to the mix, Caroline couldn't handle his teasing foreplay no longer.   With both her hands, she reached to the back of his head and pulled him in hard and assuredly.   The moment of affirmed landing was met with an impromptu thrust of verve and impulse as Caroline reflexively jolted her hips foreword to meet with Jack's lips at the place she intended to get the most self gratification.   With little resistance, Jack accepted the turn of direction willingly and most excitedly.   Licking and sucking vigorously at her pleasure zone, Jack was enjoying every second of her sweetened nectar.   The escalation of her breathing and whimpers were every bit a sign of her enjoyment. Jack's devotion to his wife was immeasurable. There was nothing he wouldn't do for his wife.   But offering such oral pleasure was just as exciting for him as it was for her.   He gained just as much pleasure form hearing her breathless pants and gasps as he played with her naked body lain in front of him. With his fingers roaming freely over her breasts, his mouth and warm tongue continued with a sultry play over her swollen excitement.

Growing with added wetness and heat, Caroline's impulse to thrust her hips into his face escalated with every fleeting second.

The passage of his efforts was slow at the very first.   But like Revel's Bolero, Jack's movements slowly picked up the rhythm with more and more energy.   As he kept perfect cadence, Caroline reacted and responded accordingly.   For several longing minutes, he effectively brought her to the brink of orgasm and brought her back down only to tease some more, and play with her brimming exhilaration.   He had her writhing and squirming in every direction.   Had they not been confined to the surrounding of a vehicle with a young child just a few feet away, she would have been loudly showing her appreciation for Jack's devotional skills.   As it were, she had enough trouble covering her mouth with a pillow to muffle the moans and groans that eventually did manage to escape her control.   At a final moment of total surrender and maximum foreplay, Jack rose from his knees and inserted his throbbing, erection into her.   His swell was maximized at an all time girth as his heart pounded with the anticipation of the first insertion; the very first thrust when passing into the warmth and wetness that can only be defined as pure animalistic ecstasy. Upon the entry and his steady guidance onward, Caroline's reflex acted accordingly by thrusting upward to meet with impulsive drive.   His shaft drove to it's limits by way of her forceful efforts. His manly parts filled her womanly body to a perfect fit.   Her every pleasure zone was met with ample supply.   As Jack continued with a pleasurable slow motion, Caroline was too far along to allow for a slow motion thrust.   With all her might and inner strength, she grabbed hold of his buttocks with both hands and pulled him closer and harder.   With a thrashing joust, she moved herself along his length in frantic spasmodic jolts and humps.   The shocks of the van began to squeal as she rocked her body in quick motion.   Her panting become more prominent once again, as she covered her face with the pillow hoping to keep from shouting allowed uncontrollably. She was quick to rouse as only seconds had passed. At the brink of her euphoric summit, Jack could read the signs of her limit, and responded accordingly. Using the weight of his body centered at his hips, he took her hard and thrust with equal effort, hard and quick to meet with her own movements. At the last second, he took hold of her hardened nipples and squeezed them just slightly. It took no time for her to achieve maximum pleasure from his efforts. Nearly out of breath and spent of any more energy, Caroline let out a squeal even the pillow couldn't have completely muffled. Her orgasm was powerful and extremely wet. *'Whoever said women don't experience sprays of orgasmic fluids was a clown with little understanding of the female anatomy.'* Caroline had left a wet spot on the van's sofa bed equal to the size of a cup of coffee. But Jack didn't stop there with his efforts to please her further and reach his own orgasm. He continued past her threshold of excitement. Pushing the envelope of her overdrive, Jack was selfishly thrusting and humping hard into her, challenging the hard working springs of the van. As her multiple orgasm continued on for a few more seconds, the wetness added to Jack's own pleasures. The slapping, slurping and suction sounds made the effect ever more exciting for the both of them.

Caroline could feel Jack was ready to pour his own juices inside her. With little energy in reserve, she managed to give Jack quite a show of her own by allowing him to see her free moving breasts sway and wave in every direction. She moved her body just right to gain the most movement with every thrusting surge. The girl was a master at pleasing her man. She understood exactly what drove him crazy. The show was most effective as his eyes concentrated heavily on her white, fleshy, rhythmic motion. Emitting a guttural grunt, Jack let lose all inhibitions and released his load. With each surging spasm, he thrust himself that much harder into her bringing her to another summit of her own.   Together they bit into the pillow making every effort to smother the feral animal that shouted from within the both of them.   Jack laid his body against hers, moving the pillow aside.   After more kisses and passionate fondling of certain body parts, the two eventually went for a second round.

Eighty-seven minutes of sexual pleasures continued until they both tired from pure exhaustion. It was never clear if all efforts to muffle their sounds and movements were effective enough to keep from waking Little El, as nothing was ever mentioned. The two lovers laid in the sofa bed with spent energies and libidos still ready for action, but they understood that at some time, the crew would be arriving expecting to leave as soon as possible. After making minimal effort to clean up, they dressed and cuddled together in an insuperable embrace.   It was every memory Caroline hung on to most from her past; securely held in his embrace, and the sultry fragrance of his expensive cologne.   After a few minutes of promising pillow talk, the two laid quietly together waiting for the monitor to show the arrival of the crew.   Without a care in the world, they relaxed and enjoyed the solidarity.   Truly, Caroline was considering her deepest desires to move back with her husband.   No doubt, Little El would have wanted nothing more for her birthday.   Before making any committal agreements, Caroline only hinted of the possibility to Jack.   Though nothing was set in stone, he accepted that much as a promising start toward a family reunion.   And that, of course, was what Jack wanted, and nothing more. Feeling content and relaxed, Jack and Caroline enjoyed holding each other, touching and caressing. It wouldn't be too long before they made a crucial mistake in judgment.   The two of them fell asleep. Making matters worse, when getting dressed, Jack's cell phone had fallen out of his pocket without his noticing.   He never heard the phone ring.

Chapter Twenty-three
Out of Revenge

As directed, the crew showed up, but not with the intentions Jack was expecting.   The occupants never saw the approaching soldiers in the monitor. And to add insult to injury, Caroline never set the motion detector on the camera knowing the movement of the van would set off the alarm's buzzer waking Little El.

They approached cautiously, not knowing what to expect from the notorious duo.   Heavily armed with automatic weapons; mini Uzi SMG, they crept up to position.   Working as a team, the soldiers silently counted down from three.   At mark zero and all at once, the glass of the side door blasted into shards and projectiles as the gun was fired at the glass to gain access into the van.   Working quickly, and most efficiently, the soldiers opened the van door by gaining access through the broken window, and forced their way inside with little opposition. Before Jack and Caroline could account for what was happening, they had been overcome by the rival gang that aspired to get even out of revenge for the death of Big Mike.   The second shot fired was from Caroline's Glock 30 as she cut down the man responsible for blasting the glass and entering the van first.   The man was forcefully thrown back by the stopping power of the .45 caliber pistol.   In an instant, Caroline and Jack were met with the muzzles of three gang members all ready to rapid fire if necessary.   As fortune would shine upon them, the soldiers were given explicit orders not to allow for, or provoke, any blood shed.   They had a mission to carry out, and murder wasn't on the list, this time. As Caroline could see the obvious futility in opposing the soldiers, she was forced to relinquished her pistol.   The ominous feeling of having three sub machine guns pointed at ones face makes for good persuasion to live to fight another day.   Seriously outnumbered, Jack and Caroline resigned themselves to listen to the demands the leader had yet to reveal. With one soldier holding his hand over El's mouth, keeping her from screaming, Jack looked to his daughter motioning not to worry.   The poor little thing was in pure panic mode.   Her eyes were wide and full of fear; the very scenario that makes for bad nightmares of the worst kind.   Once the grunts secured the van, one very familiar face made his debut.

Anthony Betuchelli was all too proud and happy to make his appearance.   "Got you two in a bit of a situation, did we?"   His sarcasm was only equaled by his ignorance.   "See what happens when junior gets passed over?   I didn't want it to happen this way, Jack, but you and your pompous family forced me into this career change."   Two of the other gun toting thugs thought it fit to laugh in fitting support.

"What do you want, Tony?"   Jack tried to reason as calmly as he possibly could.

"It's not what I'm after, Jack.   I'm just the messenger.   My new--"

"And you will always be just the messenger." Jack snidely remarked recognizing the fact that Tony had orders to keep the injuries to a minimum.

"At least the pay is better."   Tony reasoned, trying his best to sound as though her were holding the winning hand in a poker game.

"I don't doubt that's what the last baggiano (Dumbfuck) said.   Don't you realize these guys are using you, Tony.   Guys like you are expendable, you sciagurato (fool).   Just a pawn on a game board."   Jack said, knowing, only too well, what Tony would never learn in an entire lifetime.

Limited by his education and ability to think for himself, Tony simply laughed in reply as he struggled to retort.   "I doubt expendable people get paid as many Bennies as I have scored already for my contributions, Jack.   I have come to find out the grass really is greener on the other side.   Perhaps, one day you might join us.   I'm sure there are plenty of openings for your line of work." Tony's smug comment was insulting as it was based on ignorance.

Jack clearly understood that Tony hadn't been in the game long enough to know how it is played. "You have no idea what you are getting yourself into Tony." Jack warned.

"Okay enough with the small talk." Said a man, making his way through the number of soldiers surrounding the van. "For exchange of the little girl--"

Caroline screamed before he was able to give his instructions. "You wont touch my little girl." Caroline seethed with fury and maternal instincts on high alert.

"Who are you?" Jack protested trying to get the attention off of his wife.

"I'm sorry. Shame on my and my poor manners." Said the man who was well dressed in an expensive suit, unbefitting for such a motley crew of thugs and turncoats. My handle is Little Chief. And I am your worst nightmare…if you don't follow my instructions to a Tee…"

Jack listened intently, understanding his mannerism to be in charge and well versed in warfare politics. "And those instructions would be?"

"Simple, really. Wait for the call on this phone…" Little Chief placed a cell phone on the carpeted floor of the van. "Listen to the man on the other end, pay the ransom, and you get the kid back in one piece." His tone was undeniably confident and most certain to be in possession of the upper hand.

Jack grabbed Caroline at the shoulders, staying her from making any advances to harm the man. With her furious eyes sending messages of death, it would have been like her to lose diplomacy, charge the guy and tear him to shreds with her last dying breath.   Fortunately, Jack had been trained in such circumstances.   He knew the ropes well, and was confident that El would not be harmed.   There was no doubt that Jack was feeling just as angry with himself and the situation, but acting out impetuously without proper support would have been an act of suicide.   Pauly and the family support would pay any amount necessary to protect those in danger.

Caroline was frantic as the thugs took hold of El who was petrified with fear.   "They wont hurt you, baby…"   Mommy called out to her daughter. "they wouldn't dare…"   Caroline looked Little Chief directly in the eyes with absolutely no fear in her manner, grit her teeth and growled,   "I will hunt down every one of you fuckers, and I kill you myself. That's a promise, Little Chief."   Making her point quite clear, Caroline was nearly steaming with fury as the thugs made their exit in single file, taking Little El and the body of their fallen comrade with them.

But before Little Chief departed, he made the one classic mistake of turning to face Caroline. With confidence and total contempt for a mother's seethe, Little Chief blew Caroline an arrogant kiss.

If Jack hadn't taken her gun from her, she would have blown him away right there without a second thought.   For all those involved, especially Little El, it was good thing Jack was already two steps ahead of her.

As the thugs departed, Jack searched his pocket for his cell phone only to find it was missing. It was all he could do to restrain Caroline and find her cell phone to make his urgent call.   Not until every one of the gang's vehicles were out of sight did Caroline let up from her hysterical screams of tirade. Thankfully, Jack had the state of mind to remember the license plate number of the lead car.   After getting a hold of Pauly, Jack learned his dad had been frantically trying to get in touch with them for the past several hours.   Pauly's news of caution had, unfortunately come too late, but not too late to act upon accordingly.   Jack had given his dad the license plate number and a full description of the Black, Lincoln Little Chief was driving.   While the conversation with Pauly was taking place, Caroline was still in a fit of hysterics pounding her fist against the side of the van.   Just like Jack, she was infuriated with herself for having let down her guard, for having fallen asleep, and for having allowed herself to feel comfortable.   Had she been on her own, it might have been a different outcome.   Now, she must deal with the fact that they have her daughter.   The ultimate loss, second only to certain death, is kidnapping.   Nothing could cause Caroline more grief than the pain she was suffering from the moment the thugs shot out the van's window. Caroline never actually simmered down from her rant, however she did manage to listen in on what Jack was reporting to his dad.

After Jack hung up the phone, he wasted little time instructing Caroline to get into the van and find his phone.   She used her phone to call his, hoping to hear it vibrate.   The very moment she located it behind the sofa bed, Jack instructed her to hold on. With little warning, he started and revved the engine, flooring the accelerator and headed back to the main highway, tossing Caroline to and fro.   Once she regained her balance and was able to strap herself in the front passenger seat, she demanded an explanation from him.

"Who is this Tony character?   And how did he know where my daughter would be, Jack?" Caroline snarled, shedding no more tears, only a bitter ranker of anger.

"He was once one of my dad's crew

members."   Jack answered, reaching to grab his phone from Caroline.   He punched in a phone number and waited to hear from the other end.

"And your dad didn't know this Tony fool was making plans to steal my child?"

"Our child, baby.   She's mine too."   Jack got through to the other party on the phone.   "Yes, this is Jack.   I have the numbers right here.   Hold on…"   Whoever was on the other line, was already waiting to hear from Jack.   Without hesitation Jack was giving co ordinance from his cell phone.   Next, Jack was reporting the direction back to the main highway.   "You are looking for seven vehicles probably heading north at a high rate of speed.   The SUV of interest is the black Lincoln."   Apparently, the guy on the other end already had the license plate number from Pauly.   "I only have about two more miles before we lose him to merging traffic, so you'll need to get on it ASAP."

As Jack navigated quickly and swerved through the light traffic on the streets, Caroline could faintly hear the guy reporting back with negative results.   It didn't take long before she realized, Jack was relying on recourses she never knew existed.

"I am betting they will be taking the 146 to the 15 North."   Jack announced as his free hand was busy working the GPS of the van.   Seeming in control and collected, Jack showed a state of calm, Caroline could not imagine.   Like a finely tuned machine, Jack kept his mind on each task at hand without falter.   "We are less than forty-five seconds behind in a white van with chrome racks on the top." Jack continued to report the status.

Caroline not being able to clearly hear the voice on the other end of the phone was causing quite an aggravation that festered in her gut.   But the moment a positive report came over the horn, Jack showed an elated promise in his voice.

"Thank God." Jack announced. "Turning West on 146. Got it." Jack reflected, sounding positive and robotic.

"Is it El?" Caroline demanded to know the status of her daughter as well.

Without answering Caroline, Jack hit the speaker button allowing her to hear both sides of the conversation. And maneuvered through traffic.

The voice soon reported that the Black Lincoln was heading North on the 15 with only four cars in caravan. Apparently, three of the crew had broken off from the job to an undisclosed direction.

Acting accordingly, Jack used Caroline's cell to call his dad at once. He gave Pauly the progress of the activity. Pauly assured Jack that as long as the vehicles were still in rout on the road, no harm would come to El. Pauly also advised that he keep a fair distance from the kidnappers. He assured Jack that the modern equipment that they were using would not lose them. After a few more instructions and a bit of calming words, the discussion was concluded. As Jack hung up the phone, a deafening silence seemed to pervade the van.

"How are you able to follow those gang bangers?" Caroline took advantage of the silence, demanding Jack respond to her.

"Satellite." Jack replied, not taking his eyes from the road. He was in work-mode, offering little time or effort to share pleasantries in conversation as he concentrated on the road and any instructions the Satellite observer might offer.

Caroline thought a moment. Putting pieces of the puzzle together, she just realized how Jack was able to find her when she first left him. With such technology on their side, there was little anyone could do to hide from them.

"What is the Mileage range on this van between fill-ups?"   Jack asked Caroline, while writing out figures on a piece of paper.

"Four-hundred twenty-five miles."   Caroline reported, knowing exactly how well the van performed in such capacity.

Jack jotted some numbers and reported to the voice on the phone, "I now have a three-hundred eighteen mile range.   I will need to know exactly when they stop to refuel."   Jack instructed to the voice on his phone.

Caroline noticed that the van's gas gauge was reading three quarters full.

"10-4"   The voice announced, falling back into silence.

Each half hour on the road, Jack reported their exact location to Pauly.   It became apparent to Caroline through one-sided conversations that Pauly had sent much of his crew to intercept the kidnappers as long as Jack could keep his distance without being spotted.   The only missing puzzle piece was trying to guess where the kidnappers might be taking El. If their turf was back toward South Dakota, they took a slight chance of losing the kidnappers in the dark of night.

A few minutes later, splitting through the silence, the voice came over the speaker announcing that the four vehicles had changed direction onto Highway 95.

Jack acknowledged, reporting that he was only a mile behind that interchange.   He then called Pauly to report the change of direction.   Working like a multi-processing machine, Jack was using every advantage afforded to him at the helm of the van with the GPS, the satellite tracker and two cell phones at his disposal.   This was, obviously, Jack's expertise, Caroline had never before witnessed.

Whoever was doing the monitoring of the kidnappers was a vigilant operator.   Caroline was feeling far more grateful understanding that her family had such advanced technological resources. But she continued to ring her hands in anger.   The idea of her innocent little girl in the hands of those heartless monsters made her feel incredibly evil and less apt to offer them any pity once she reached her daughter.

Another half hour past when Jack called Pauly reporting the new location.   Obviously, the kidnappers were making haste, traveling as quickly as they could.

The next time the voice came over the speaker, he reported the thugs had stopped at a station for fuel.   Jack did the same a mile back, doing his best to top off the tanks in the time allotted before the thugs got back on the road to resume their travels.   Calculating that the van carried enough fuel to travel nearly twice the distance as the crew, he felt confident that a getaway could be possible if they chose to continue to use the van in the pursuit.   And knowing that the crew chose to use Highway 95, he was betting that a successful interception could be made on that same highway if they were to gain the distance on them with Pauly's crew.   It wasn't until he had stopped for fuel that Jack spoke to Caroline directly.   He wasn't weaving through traffic nor preoccupied with conversation when Caroline attempted to have a dialogue with him.   She had never seen him behaving so strangely before.   No doubt, they were both under the horrible stress of losing their child to unpredictable kidnappers.   But something else was eating away at him.   Caroline knew that at that moment she could make an effort to talk to him without inhibiting his search for El.   As the numbers on the fuel pump continued to rack up with Jack manning the nozzle in one hand, and his cell phone in the other, Caroline approached cautiously, putting her hands around his waist.   He seemed surprised that she had made such a move.

"Hey, it's me, Jack."   Caroline tried to calm his tense nerves.   "We will get her back.   I have confidence in you."   Hearing herself saying the words also helped to slightly calm her own agitation.

Jack took a moment to reply.   He seemed distant and noncommittal.   "I am so sorry, Caroline."   Jack nearly melted as the first words pored from his mouth.   "This is my fault."   He said barely able to make eye contact with her.

Caroline realized the sudden change in Jack was all based on guilt.   "There is no fault or blame, Jack, only solution.   You deal with that bastard Tony, and I will deal with that character, Little Bitch."

"First things first, we will need to know where our little girl is going.   Then we will work on a plan of attack."   Jack assured her, he understood the nature of this kind of business.

"Then I blow a hole in that cocky son of a bitch."   Said Caroline, denoting a serious side he had never before seen in her.

Jack fondly stared at his wife a moment.   "I have seen that look in only one other woman in my life, and she is married to my brother."

"I guess this shit runs in the family."   Caroline smirked similar to the Crystal's signature smile.

"I guess so…"   Said Jack, scratching his head in wonderment.   In the back of Jack's mind he was comparing the two girls and taking notice of the distinct similarities in their personalities.   He justified that two brothers could be very much alike by way of choosing very similar women in their lives.

Suddenly, the voice over the phone made an announcement. "It looks like they are ready to hit the road Jack."

"10-4." Jack replied, shutting off the gas pump and replacing the nozzle back in the receptacle. Jack paused before jumping back in the van, and reached for Caroline. "I love you, and I promise you, we *will* get our daughter back if it's the last thing I do, she will be back with you." Jack was more than just being optimistic.

"With *us*. She will be back with us. They have no idea what they are up against." Caroline confidently announced, as she accepted Jack's help into the van. Wasting no time, they were back on the road coordinating their distance with the kidnappers. And again, Jack called his dad, reporting the location in hope to get the back up needed to gain back Little El, and put an end to Tony's personal vendetta against the family.

While on the road after getting fuel, Jack was more talkative. His guilt riddled mind was less stressed out after Caroline made it clear that he had no control over what Tony was thinking when he conjured up such a devious plan to kidnap a child from Pauly's family. At the time of the kidnapping, Jack seriously thought that Caroline was angry with him for allowing such a heinous crime to take place. His own self-guilt had evoked feelings of inadequacies in matters of protection. It never crossed his mind that she was simply angry with herself for dropping her own guard. It was then, Jack realized that Caroline wasn't privy to the certain details of the case. And he took the extra time needed to choose his words wisely as not to worry Caroline anymore than she was already. "It has just occurred to me that you might not have recognized the one your refer to as, Little Bitch."

Caroline looked to Jack with curiosity written all over her face.   She had yet to weigh the gravity of the situation. "Should I have?"

"I'm just going to tell you straight out so you know what we are up against, Caroline."   Jack paused a moment to catch his breath, realizing there really was no easy way to break the news to her. "He's Big Mike's little brother."   Jack announced, dropping the bombshell over her head as softly as he could.   "This fiasco of Tony's is not his game. Tony was simply the patsy who dropped the dime on you and me, I'm sorry to say.   We simply got caught in our own snare, so to speak.   When my dad called for extra protection for us, he inadvertently called Tony and his band of thugs into play.   None of this would have happened if Tony hadn't been demoted in rank for being the fool that he is.

Caroline looked to have changed by two shades of grey.   The pulsing heart rate in her neck became more prominent and pronounced, as her breathing became labored and unsteady.   Her mind was whirring with every horrible thought that came with the memories of Big Mike and his relentless thugs.   But instead of cowering in a corner or showing an ounce of fear, Caroline straightened up in her seat and began to formulate her own theory and plan of attack.   "What other intel to you have for me?"   She asked, boldly searching for any weakness she could use to her advantage.

"Very little, I'm afraid.   They are well organized, as you already know.   And they mobilized very quickly.   We have yet to find the main chieftain, however.   We thought, at first, that Big Mike was the boss man.   But we found out differently just recently.   We suspect that Little Chief is now second in command to whom may be another brother.   Word on the street is very hushed, they keep his name and identity very quiet.   Until we find where he hides out, it will be difficult to extinguish this resilient group of thugs.

"Quite a bees nest…"   Caroline murmured aloud, half expected to be heard, as she stared ahead looking to be fighting back her own fears.

"Yes, quite.   But it's okay, babe.   We will stir it up and cause him to surface.   I'm sure you realize now that Tony has changed sides, we have no idea how much information he has given them.   We can only assume the worst, and act accordingly. One fortunate factor remains to our advantage is that Tony has no idea where we are traveling   or why. For these very reasons, the last-string players are never given such information."   Jack said, showing his mind set as pragmatic and calculating.   "When we get El back, and we *will*, rest assured, every effort will be made to assure your safety.   The family will do everything to continue to protect the two of you. But I have reason to believe our last stand will conclude very soon."   Jack stated with his mind still calculating strategies and counter attacks.

"All I did was walk into a tiny, Podunk convince store, and this is what develops from simply wanting to live."   Caroline subdued.

"And you are here today as proof that thugs like them wont be tolerated in our society.   You are a survivor, a good soldier and a warrior.   Few could have done what you pulled off and lived to see another day.   And you saved more than just one life. Your walking into that store on that fateful day was simply unfortunate.   But you survived, and you learned how to handle yourself while understanding that certain measures of protection must be taken in order to keep peace.   There are thousands of pacifist out there who would rather lay down and simply die at the hands of the criminals rather than stand up and fight for their rights to fight back."   Jack sought the opportunity to justify his beliefs and those of his family by informing Caroline exactly how he felt. "America was founded on the rights to bear arms. It's the second amendment in our constitution.   And yet, so many foolish Americans honestly believe that gun control would stop the violence.   Little do any of those fools understand that gun control only puts guns in the hands of the criminals.   I can guarantee that none of those Israeli issued Uzi's were rightfully registered by those thugs.   I can also guarantee that no properly registered gun owner has ever walked into a school or restaurant and committed murder. Yet, all those nearsighted lobbyists and twofaced bureaucrats have nothing better to do than work against hard working citizens while disarming them, and then expecting them to fend for themselves.   It is so unfortunate that many have no idea what they are talking about as they fight for gun control.   It saddens me to think that it should even be an issue. Since America was first founded, gun rights were entered into our amended rights.   I may not have been born in this country, but I am sure as hell proud to be here, and I will fight to maintain that right.   I know that you may not understand my political stance at this time, but rest assured, if it were not for certain vigilantes -- for lack of a better word -- and private sectors of interests, such as ours, this country would not and could not have come this far up the echelon of power.   Private industry made this country what it is today.   And there are far more private sectors ready, willing and able to protect our rights as human beings and American.   And those unsanctioned citizens like crooked politicians, gangs and such criminals willing to disrupt the way of business will swiftly suffer the consequences."

Jack's winded speech seemed to be something he never had the chance to voice aloud to Caroline in the past.   It simply never came up.

"From my cold dead hand."   Caroline commented, showing her support for her husband's staunch beliefs.

"You got that right, sister."   Jack commended.

"Amen…"   The voice said, from Jack's cell phone.

Chapter Twenty-four
Warfare

The excursion across the state of Nevada continued on up to Reno before showing signs of slowing.   By which time, Pauly's cavalry had long caught up to the race.   With the aid of the man monitoring the satellite dish in space, Jack and the rest of the joining crew were able to follow from afar without being detected.   It was unfortunate that Pauly's crew had to backtrack nearly two-hundred miles, but who knew?   It was everything Pauly could do to protect his family at the mere expense of a few extra gallons of gas.

        Once it was discovered exactly where the thugs had taken El, it was just a matter of minutes for Jack and his crew to organize a plan of attack. According to the satellite operator, the crew would have to work quickly.   It was understood that the thugs were only stopping to stock up on supplies as he witnessed them loading and unloading items from each of the cars.   One last call was made to Pauly from Jack as he informed his father that loved him very much.   He also gave Pauly the coordinates of the place the thugs brought El.   The entire conversation was only seconds, and yet, the long drive to the destination seemed like a painful eternity without El.   With the satellite guy on standby after he had given every bit of helpful information available to him, Jack instructed the crew to act accordingly.   They had a good idea as to the layout of the stop off place, thanks to the eye in the sky. Only two other cars where already parked at the location denoting less than ten additional soldiers to fight against.   At best, Jack was able to figure that the enemy had no more than thirty thugs to contend with.   The property of interest had no alley access from the back.   Nor did it have any blind spots to park and convene.   The attack would have to be fast and hard, making it vitally important to keep El from harm while commencing in her rescue.   The element of surprise was all they had as their first and primary tactic to use.   Then Jack came up with a idea.

According to the satellite guy, El was never removed from the car.   In fact, most of the thugs remained in the other three cars while the drones from the house helped to load the supplies.   Their organization was well orchestrated with good leadership skills.   It was unfortunate that they were the enemy and not allies.

"How much insurance did you take out on this van?"   Jack asked Caroline most seriously.

"More than enough.   What's your plan?" Caroline was already placing the extra Glock in her waistband, and a police issue, compact Berretta 9mm in her ankle holster.

Jack smirked in answer.   "Got an idea." Jack and the entire backup crew parked only a quarter mile from the site as he figured out a plan.   From his overnight bag, Jack removed what looked like a package of regular chewing gum.   Then he used what looked like a shoe lace to insert the aglet (the end of the lace) into the package of gum.   The other end of the aglet was inserted into what looked like an ordinary alarm clock.

Caroline looked to be astonished by such intriguing camouflage.   "C-4 made to look like chewing gum?"

"Never leave home without gum that goes bang."   Jack announced, as his crew gathered around the van awaiting for final instructions.   In less than ten seconds, Jack rallied the plan that suited the topography.   Like a huddled football team, each member dispersed at once, quickly taking position. Jack and Caroline emptied the van of all their property, and packed everything into the other cars. Next, they took the van with all the members following closely behind in their cars.   They set up just out of eye shot from the site.   The point of angle that Jack needed was too difficult to accomplish.   So he parked the van on the lawn of one of the neighbor houses just three doors down.   He set the alarm clock for thirty seconds then quickly placed it and the fake gum beneath the driver's seat. Using the curtain rope,   he then tied the steering wheel to the turn signal making sure the trajectory of the vehicle remained straight. With Caroline and the entire crew hidden behind the cover of the van, Jack gave the signal as he dropped the van's shift handle into drive. Slowly, the van pulled forward across the lawn of each of the neighbors.   The rolling path of the van continued as planned toward the side of the house and away from his child.   Those who were coming and going from the house would be the unfortunate ones to be wearing a van for lunch.   Each of the crew, working for Jack, were heavily armed with automatic weapons.   The climactic scene looked like a training camp exercise depicted from a soldier of fortune magazine.   Those who stepped out of their homes were quick to jump back inside. Amazingly, those that did show their faces seemed rather pleased to see a force targeted at the gang's location.   Though the thugs may have been organized amongst themselves, perhaps the gang bangers hadn't been hospitable neighbors. Nonetheless, no one gave warning of the coming attack.   And just as planned, the van gained speed heading as it was directed.   The thugs had no time to react once the van plowed through a high hedge of oleanders just one-hundred fifty feet from impact at the side of the house.   Jacks crew, including Caroline, hung back behind the remaining hedges clear of what was to come.   The loud impact of the van against the house occurred with a tumultuous commotion.   A count of four thugs came from the house to investigate.   Three of which were quick to approach the van as they attempted, unsuccessfully, to open the passenger side doors.

Jack quietly counted down as he viewed his watch.   "Five, four, three, two…bingo."

The explosion carried a blasting concussion of heated air in a wave all the way to the crew as they charged all the survivors that remained breathing or moving.   Many of Jack's crew headed straight for the cars making certain they wouldn't be able to escape the attack.   Tires and radiators were the first to be shot out.   The head count of casualties from the initial blast of C-4 took out the first three investigators, and three more that were in the house. All the grunts that were used to load and unload the cars were the immediate targets.   Most of which were too slow to retrieve their guns from their waistbands.   One thug was witnessed to have dropped his box of groceries only to lose his drawers as he attempted to free his gun from his loosely fitting pants.   He died with his baggies down around his ankles.   Another who wore his laces untied was blasted right out of his shoes as they remained in perfect place while he was launched six feet back. The last of the thugs that were on foot that managed to survive the initial hail storm of bullets and C-4 were killed in the cross fire of their own men.   Nine in all, were the first to perish.   Foolishly, those that were in the cars panicked feeling trapped in the disabled cars, reacted spontaneously by extricating themselves from the cars only to meet with the rapid fire of the crew.   Jack's experience in such warfare paid off with high dividends.   With military precision, Jack's crew carried out their orders flawlessly with expert efficiency.   The rapid fire of guns could, no doubt, be heard throughout the entire neighborhood.   Resembling a war zone, the smell of spent powder waft thick in the air as hundreds of rounds were fired in the immediate area of the site.

Caroline was the first to encounter the SUV

that housed her daughter.   Knowing that Little Chief was still inside the SUV as well, extra caution was exercised by her and the crew.   The first of three grunts exited the SUV with his gun firing indiscriminately while he tried to gain shelter behind the car door, but to no avail.   He was hit four times at point blank range.   With the SUV strategically surrounded, hands of surrender suddenly appeared through the open windows.   Taking no chances, Jack and his crew remained behind cover as he called out his instructions to the remaining occupants of the SUV.   Little Chief and one other were the last of the survivors.   The two did as they were instructed and exited the car, hands exposed and in the air.   On the other side of the SUV, crew members secured the vehicle.   After the, all clear, signal from them, Jack grabbed Little Chief, throwing him to the pavement. The other thug decided to take his chances against two dozen of Jack's crew only to lose his life without getting a single shot off.   His death was such a waste, a senseless suicide.   He never took notice that Caroline had him covered from behind.   As he reached for his gun that was hidden at the small of his back, Caroline recognized him to be the one who had initially grabbed her daughter at the kidnapping. She gave him little consideration as she open fired on him.   Offering no remorse or the least bit of compassion, Caroline proved herself steadfast and worthy in the eyes of all the crew.

All that remained was Little Chief who smugly laughed and remained defiant with Jack's commands.   It became quite clear that a clever switch had been performed and had somehow eluded the eyes in the sky.   Inside the SUV was devoid of any more souls.   The crew quickly scrambled to check each car and the house only to come up empty of Little El.   She was nowhere to be found.   With

each crew member reporting back to Jack, Little
Chief found it appropriate to laugh aloud even harder.
With his face in the pavement of the street and his
hands bound behind him via a sturdy plastic tie-wrap,
Jack interrogated him after he was searched and
found to have nothing on him that gave hint as to
where their child was taken.   He was relived of a
fancy pair of gold plated Colt, 1911's.
Unfortunately, Little Chief wasn't giving up anything
else in the way of information.   And though
Caroline wanted desperately to plug his laughing pie-
hole, Jack knew better than to kill the only remaining
leverage they had.   They needed him alive if they
expected to get El back in one piece.   Truly, the
gang bangers had played out their hand rather well by
switching El to one of the other three cars before
being detected, but Jack and Caroline weren't giving
up anytime soon.   Quickly, before the cops could
arrive, the crew gathered Little Chief and information
they found at the site then retreated back to their cars.
The resistant hostage was virtually dragged by force
as he fought tirelessly.   His arrogance and self-
righteous attitude was trying Carline's patience with
every chuckle and snide remark he would taunt.
The man showed little fear in the face of death.   No
doubt, he recognized the fact Jack would be needing
him as leverage.   However, he made if very difficult
to consider allowing him the privilege of breathing.

   Back at the cars, where Jack, Caroline and
Little Chief were expeditiously chauffeured away
from the neighborhood, Jack looked through the
index of Little Chief's cell phone.   Little
information could be gleaned from the encrypted
texts and messages.

   Jack made a call to his father informing them
of the situation.   Though he was commended by his
father for conducting a job very well done, Jack

wasn't the least bit happy due to the fact they had no idea where their daughter was being held.   Of course, Pauly understood the situation only too well, consoling Jack that they did all that they could under the circumstances.   Pauly advised the entire crew to meet up at the Indian reservation.   Knowing that each party now had equal leverage over the other, Pauly figured he would be able to persuade the trade to take place at the reservation.

Rather than tip his hand, Jack believed it was best that Little Chief's people not know what happened to them until the very last.   As far as they knew, little Chief and his thugs were probably still in transit.   So when Little Chief's cell phone rang just forty-five minutes after he had been abducted, Jack simply ignored the call.   Leaving the gang in the dark would give them a better chance of recovering their daughter.   Once they arrived at the reservation, Jack was amazed how close it was to Reno.   Both Jack and Pauly figured that the gang bangers must not be too far from a meeting place inasmuch as it only took forty-five minutes to be missed.   Now, all they could do was wait for the contact phone to ring.

In the meantime, Caroline called the police and reported her rental van stolen.   She enjoyed the irony as she gave the description of the man who stole it as Little Chief.

With nerves on edge and stomach ulcers burning away, Caroline checked on the batteries of the cell phone nearly a dozen times.   It was a horrible feeling knowing that the only binding security between her and her daughter was that cheap disposable cell phone, Little Chief had left with them. Meanwhile, Jack was organizing his men and working closely with Pauly.   The rustic condition of the reservation was dusty and similar to the setting of a western movie. It was difficult to imagine Crystal being taken to such a place to receive a miracle cure.

Crystal had been brought to a secure place where no one would think to look for her, much less find her in her weakened condition.   To her chagrin the transfer of blood from Jason Mathison had no effect on her health in the least.   Her fatigue precluded her from being able to help in any of the family matters.   As Roberto and two other crew members stayed with them, the remaining team assembled in various strategic parts of the reservation in an attempt to gain the advantage over what could be a large number of rivals.   At this point, both parties were, pretty much, in the dark as far as knowing who had the upper hand.   Even the eye in the sky was of no use since they had absolutely no idea where El was being held.

The local Tribal Police were very helpful in allowing free access to the reservation, however, they made it a point to inform Pauly they wanted nothing to do with the battle that was brewing.   In fact, the Tribal Police had their hands full, making sure that their own people were safely behind doors.   In the past, Jason had treated and cared for the native American people on that reservation many times over.   He was their chief medicine man and guide. It was Jason's word that assured the people of the reservation that none of them would be harmed. Jason had a perfect track record of previous predictions.   He was never doubted or contested for over one-hundred and fifty years.   They certainly weren't about to doubt his word now.

"If you break the phone, they wont come." Jack came up behind Caroline, hoping to calm her nerves.   Taking the contact phone from her hands, Jack put it in his pocket and turned Caroline to face him.   In his embrace, he wrapped his arms around her in an attempt to ease her worried mind.   Her thoughts were in such disarray.   Like any parent would do in such circumstances, she would think the worst, and continually worry about the pain and anguish Little El must have been going through. Just the mere thought of her little face showing signs of fear and abandonment drove Caroline to the brink of insanity.   She was given her chance to make Little Chief talk and give up her location, but he wouldn't budge from obstinate and rude behavior.

"I am so afraid she will suffer permanent damage from this horrible nightmare."   Caroline confided to Jack.

"She's a bright kid, Caroline.   She knows what's up.   She understands well enough to know, we are doing everything we can to get her back safely."   Jack rubbed her back as he spoke calmly and assuredly .   "You have done well with her. She will be fine."

"When this is all over, I personally want that bastard, Little Chief."   Caroline scowled as she grit her teeth, barely allowing the words to pass.

"And you will…I guarantee it."   Pauly announced as he appeared from inside the house. Pauly hugged the two of them showing his support for her demands.

Holding back her tears, Caroline reciprocated, pressing her head against his.   "I'm sorry all this trouble has followed me here to your family, Pauly." Caroline said with a lump in her throat and tears rolling down her face.

"Nonsense, Agness.   You *are* family. Always and forever.   And don't you forget it."   His levity in calling her by an odd name had always brought a smile to her lips, until now.   "We will get her back.   And all of them will pay for what they have caused us."   Pauly always had a way with offering positive words of hope.

Through the sniffles and tears, the three of them held the other tightly, as if to be keeping hold of El's memory.   "I just want her back.   I don't care what happens to Tony or that Little Prick."   She said, fighting back the emotions and the urge to cry aloud.

"I understand."   Pauly reported.   "And you will get her back.   I guarantee it."   Pauly's words were ever so promising, but unfortunately, under the circumstances, Caroline was not assured of anything.   There were no guarantees in the present situation.

From within the house a stranger came out. Unfamiliar to Caroline, the voice of the woman was soft yet outspoken.   "I can see your anger, Caroline."   She said with a redeeming sense of authority.

The threesome spontaneously separated as the voice broke through the momentary silence.   Pauly stepped back with an open arm and invited the young woman to come closer.   "This young lady is Sara. Sara, this is my daughter Zelda, fondly referred to as Caroline.

Caroline smiled and quipped,   "Among a dozen other strange names."   Caroline offered a friendly smile, and held out her hand to meet with Sara.   "It's nice to meet you."

"Sara is one of the tribal leaders here on the reservation.   All parties, gatherings, social events and *wars* have to go through her before it reaches the counsel.   She's a natural leader just like her grand father who was the Chief of these great people, once upon a great time."   Pauly proudly bragged, obviously very impressed with her and her family's résumé.

"Wow, it's good to see a woman in the leadership seat."   Caroline boasted her liberated stance in society.

"You are a born leader too, Caroline…" Sara replied, as she examined Caroline's palm and facial features.   "You have a strong background as well.   People like you, your sister Crystal and me are also natural leaders.   It is a good day when so many of us can gather and meet."   Sara was no palm reader, but certain physical features are always used to define people as who they truly are.

"Perhaps under different circumstances." Caroline added.

"Especially under *these* circumstances," Sara affirmed.   "Life isn't always going to be a, fun filled, party, double dipped in a chocolaty bliss. Many of us do best under pressure.   I can tell that you excel best when under fire.   That fire in your gut keeps you vigil and always alert.   Be grateful the fire keeps you up at night, and burns threefold in the presence of betrayal.   It's those signs that keep you alive and strong to fight another day."

"Wow, I really like this girl."   Said Caroline, boasting her new found friend.   "You possess quite an understanding of people.   I think we're going to get along quite nicely."   Caroline smiled as best she could under the circumstances.

Sara grinned back in reply.   "I have just one message to relay before I go.   Jason has asked me to inform you that your young, daughter Elizabeth with be fine with no residual suffering from this ordeal. She is as strong minded as you are, and she will come out of this just fine."

As if the comforting words came down from God himself, Caroline nearly melted as she hugged Sara.   "Thank you.   I truly needed to hear that." After embracing Sara, Caroline made a personal inquiry.   "How is Crystal?"   Caroline pulled away, looking deeply in Sara's dark, pretty eyes.   "Has Jason predicted that she will be fine as well?"

Without a hint of doubt, Sara assured good tidings.   "Jason has seen worse cases, and they did just fine.   Crystal is as tough as nails, and though she hasn't recovered yet, she will do just fine.   The medicine man's magic doesn't miss."   Sara said, knowing that several hours had already passed and Crystal hadn't shown any signs of recovery. Though Jason's magic was very strong and always effective, it had gone to show just how critical Crystal's illness truly was.

"I will take your word for it.   Thank you, again for allowing us to hold up here.   I hope we don't cause your people any trouble or injury." With a true sincerity, Caroline felt terrible about the trouble that was about to unfold on the reservation.

"We have fought such battle for hundreds of years.   This is nothing new to us.   We will keep our heads as long as you keep yours."   Sara smiled before biding her best wishes and went beck inside the house.

At that moment the contact cell phone rang out from within Jack's pocket.   Quick to react, Jack answered immediately.   The one-sided conversation lasted for several seconds before Jack got the chance to speak freely.   "I'm afraid that's where you are wrong, Pal."   Jack explained.   "It will be at my specified time at my specified location.   If you think five million dollars is easy to simply withdrawal and transport, your wrong.   We don't keep that kind of cash in our back pockets."   A momentary pause took place as Jack, and everyone around him, waited impatiently for a reply.   "I will give you the exact location when I hear back from you with confirmation from your boss.   Have a nice day."

Jack pressed the end button on the cheap cell phone, concluding the conversation abruptly.

Caroline nearly kicked Jack as she believed his curt conversation was overly detrimental to her daughter's safety. "How could you be so belligerent to them?   What make's you think they wont take it out on our daughter, Jack?"   Caroline was doing her best to keep from losing her temper.

Pauly pulled Caroline aside and gave her a few pointers.   "Jack has been trained by the best, sweetie.   He knows exactly how to handle these thugs.   The moment we seem weak or fearful for the hostage, they will believe they have the upper hand. Unlike the crap you see on television, we have to act as heartless as they.   We must never mention the name of the kidnapped and never make it easy for them to make the arrangements.   I am sorry to be the one to have to tell you this, but the way this plays out best is when they believe we have little empathy for the hostage or their cause.   Just as America is noted for never giving into such demands of ransom, we must act accordingly.   I know it is hard to hear, but I assure you, they will be calling back soon with an agreement of our terms."

"Are you kidding me?"   Caroline squalled. "And risk them dumping her on the side of the road because they might have felt we didn't have the heart or the money?"

Just then the contact phone rang.   Jack answered after waiting until after the third ring. "We will meet at a neutral location at an Indian reservation up North.   It is at the Lake Pyramid location just outside of Reno.   It will take us six hours to get there…"

Pauly had to grab Caroline to keep her from grabbing the phone away from Jack.

"…so give us till morning to get the money

and travel the distance." Jack waited for a reply. "Same to you." Jack hung up the phone, giving Caroline a grimacing stare.

"I know, I know…" Caroline relented. It is so hard to go another minute without her, much more, six hours." She sighed heavily wishing it was all over.

"Strategy, my love." Jack assured. "This is a chess game of strategy that we must play out to the best of our ability. We have done this before, and I assure you they are cooperating as planned, Caroline. Think about it, they have no idea that we are already here. They must be close since they never once claimed that they would need more time. Theoretically, we have given them what they think is the advantage. They will, most likely, show up here late in the night under the cover of darkness just as they did in South Dakota. And thinking confidently, they will meet with our guys and deadly consequences at every turn." Jack knew he was making perfect sense to his wife. He also understood that she wasn't on her own turf which made her feel very uncomfortable. He figured, in time, she would learn to adjust to the impromptu situations.

Caroline looked to Pauly who was nodding and showing her that Jack was well versed in such matters. Pauly had every confidence in his son's warfare strategy. "Do we have the money if all goes awry?" Caroline addressed her question directly to Pauly who was obviously the patriarch and the officiate.

"Pocket change, sweetie. Of course we have that kind of money in our back pocket. We just don't admit it to anyone." Pauly assured confidence and proper management of the situation.

Not being accustomed to such tactics and

psychology, Caroline took it well as she began to learn the ropes of a new kind of warfare up close and personal.   "Thank you, Pauly."   Caroline relented soberly.   "I don't know how you guys can be so cool under pressure like this.   I fell like I'm about to explode."

"We are too."   Pauly announced.   "It's just a matter of bluffing and not showing the fear.   I assure you, this is the only way to get her back safely."

Chapter Twenty-five
Perdition

Caroline never slept or rested long enough to make a difference in her performance.   She couldn't have been more ready to face the opposition, rested or not.   Jack spent much of his time talking and strategizing with many of the crew.   And they spent much of their time anticipating a surprise encounter as Jack had predicted.   The gang would most likely scout out the terrain and place their soldiers at various places to gain some advantage. Well practiced in such battles, Jack had armed his entire crew with the right tools for the right battle. Money was no object as far as family, and the protection of family was concerned.   Each of Pauly's soldiers were equipped with night vision goggles and powerful crossbows.   Quieter than silencers, crossbows are a stealthy weapon in darkness.

As it became a waiting game, most were simply keeping vigil while others were give the chance to rest in shifts.   So far, as Jack had explained to Caroline, the gang bangers were already playing into their own catastrophic end.   The mere fact that Jack had called the meeting place, gave them the battlefront advantage.   From miles away, Jack's people could see anyone coming.   The dark of night fell upon the sable desert with little moonlight to take place.   The sky was filled with shimmering stars the city people could never imagine existed.   Even the silence of the desert offered a peaceful calm that lent a hand in preparing for battle.

Everyone was on high alert when the first call came from the scout at the gate.   Several of the gang members arrived early in the darkness as predicted by Jack.   They approached cautiously, many of which split into several groups.   Judging by the maximum number each car could carry, scouts had figured that nearly seventy five gang members had come to face the battle.

Fortunately, Jack was correct on every account.   Soon after the gang bangers arrived at the front gate, many had gone on foot to seek out high ground above the center of town.   Numerous the thugs were too far from the action to know what was about to take place.   They had no idea of the terrain or the size of the opposition.

Taking no chances, Pauly had ordered no prisoners or hostages.   "Those who sneak around in the dark with deadly weapons shall see and receive just what they came for."

An hour after the gang bangers had first arrived, the light of dawn had barely begun to peek over the distant hills.   The gang bangers waited seven hours before the next contact.   Needless to say, Caroline was nearly crawling out of her skin with anxieties and worry for her young daughter. Already, team leaders had reported in with counts of casualties inflicted on the opposition.   The stealthy silence of the arrows worked wonders giving the gang bangers no reason for alarm.   Already, the gang bangers had lost twenty-six in Reno, and another twelve up in the hills of the reservation, and the lead guy had no idea what he was dealing with.

When the next call came, the man introduced himself as Trey.   This would be the first time anyone from Pauly's investigators had heard this name.   The progression of events moved rather swiftly once Trey agreed to meet with Jack and Pauly at the center of town.   One of Pauly's team was instructed to retrieve Trey and bring him to the meeting place.   All the while Carline was fully aware that Little El was probably only a few yards from her the whole time they waited for the phone call.

More than a dozen cars of every make and model trialed into the center of the reservation.   No two cars looked alike, and none of them looked to be bullet proof or protected in any way.   Nonetheless, the cars were lead into the very place Jack felt most comfortable to conduct business.   As protocol, and one last precautionary measure, Jack made one quick call to his pal with the eyes in the sky.

The morning light was a bit hazy and chilled. The rise of the Easterly sun hadn't peeked the hills or the houses yet.   The gang bangers exited their cars, all fully armed with automatic weapons and similar attire as those who apposed them and died at the Reno location.   How odd, Caroline thought, that these men, most of which were barely eighteen years of age, chose to wear their clothes in such a sloppy manner that should they need to run for their lives, they would first, need to pull up there pants so their legs might be able to stretch maybe a half-stride. Nevertheless, their attitude and righteous stance proved that they felt that not only did they have the upper hand, but they seemed to feel indestructible as they toted their guns like flashy jewelry.

As a show of leadership (or some form of self-righteousness), Trey dialed the contact phone one last time.   As Jack answered the phone, Trey was seen tossing the phone aside into the dirt on the street.   Apparently, he wanted to know who he had been talking with previously.   As Jack hung up the phone, and placed it back in his pocket, he stood and waited for the man to approach him.   Trey never showed fear or any regard for his safety as he appeared to approach without a gun in his hand.   He most probably had his heat packed in his waistband hidden by the long, leather duster he wore.   He walked slow and confidently with both arms crossed at the wrists.   His minion thugs, however, were trigger happy and only too eager to shed some blood, in hope of gaining some points with the boss.   From fifty feet away, Trey opened his mount to speak, proving he was, in fact, the one that Jack was speaking to previously.   "You have the money?" Trey's arrogance was only second to Little Chief's.

"Where is the girl?"   Jack demanded, never

revealing she was his daughter.

Trey snapped his fingers like he was the protagonist of some cheap, B rated movie.   From the car behind him, Anthony Betuchelli exited from the back seat.   He was wearing a similar leather duster, obviously working as an understudy, trying to emulate his boss.   He reached into the car and pulled and tugged until a little figure of a person emerged with a hood over her head and her hands tied behind her back.   The fact she was resisting and able to walk on her own proved she wasn't seriously harmed.   Of course, Tony being the tough guy that he thought he was, felt it appropriate to forcibly push the young prisoner along.   Once she was in place, along side Trey and Tony, Jack pointed to the large briefcase that was set on the porch.

Right away, Trey ordered Tony to retrieve the briefcase.   Upon doing so, the hood was removed from the child's head.   And Tony managed to disappear into the crowd of the other thugs.

Showing no apparent injuries or trauma, El looked to be in good sprits considering her horrific ordeal.   It took several seconds for her eyes to acclimate to the light, but once she saw her dad standing opposite her and the thugs, her face lit up with assured confidence.

As Trey opened the case and fingered through some of the stacks of clean new bills, he appeared to be very pleased.   A gloating cow-eyed stare seemed to prevail for a few seconds before gaining back his sense of mission.

Jack held out his hand encouraging his daughter to come over to his side.

Fortunately, all went well with the transaction.   Little El was safely delivered to her dad, and was quickly whisked away into the house by several of the crew that were standing by.

"Everything seem in order?"   Jacked called out, ready for phase two of his plan.

Trey nodded and smiled.   "For now…I still have business with the kid's mother.   Ya know, an eye for an eye sort of thing."   Acting cocky and smooth as mud, Trey was determined to even the score.   Apparently, the money was only a bonus and a way to prove to his team members that he was in complete control.

"That's not going to happen, Trey.   You got what you came for.   I think it's time you and your posse leave here while you can still breathe on your own."   Jack said rather calmly and suggestively.

Unfortunately, Trey wasn't the type to be told what to do, regardless of the fact a good many of Jack's men were determined to cut Trey and his thugs down.   Trey looked to the ground and shook his head as he opened his jacket revealing a decent arsenal in his waistband.   "I think ya'll are missing the point.   Big Mike would want retribution.   I believe he deserves retribution."   Trey opened his hands and simply replied,   "Just send the bitch my way and everybody lives happily ever after."   Trey instructed, actually believing that Jack would do as asked because that was how proper business was conducted among leaders.

"It's not going to happen.   But I can guarantee that you will be the first to die if you continue to act irrational."   Jack offered a tone of bantering resolve.

"Fuck this…"   Trey bellowed with anger in his eyes.   He reached for his gun and pointed it directly at Jack.   "Bring the bitch to me, or we all die."   A loud chatter of shifting guns took place as everyone braced for war.

Just then, a familiar voice was calling out to Trey.   "This is the bitch that killed Big Mike!"

Immediately, Trey recognized the voice but could not see where it was coming from. "Where you at?" Trey looked around, certainly not expecting to hear his brother's voice.

"Little Bitch is right here." Caroline said, shoving Little Chief to the ground who was bound at the hands and ankles. The shackles that loosely bound his legs made it difficult for him to fully stride as Caroline shoved him along into the street.

In an instant, everyone was taking aim and readying their firearms for war. Trey was fit to leap over all the cars just to tear into Caroline who was only too eager to see him try.

"Just shoot the dumb bitch, Trey." Little Chief hadn't yet observed the fact that they were heavily outnumbered. Regardless of the fact, it hadn't yet become common knowledge that Trey's scouting team were already casualties of war.

"Yeah, just shoot the Little Bitch." Caroline retorted spitefully, as she took aim at Little Chief's head. "What's the matter pal? Too afraid you might hit Little Weasel or whatever the hell his handle is?" Caroline looked straight at the guy daring him to try.

Those who were in the immediate area could almost see the steam coming from Trey's head as he festered and spit. "Let him go, and I'll let you have the money." Trey said, trying desperately to formulate a plan. No doubt, his greed was far too great to ignore that much money. Had it been anyone but his brother, there would have been a hailstorm of gunfire already commenced.

"Well, now your talking." Jack claimed. "Just toss the case of money to the side, and he's all yours."

Trey was quite hesitant to do as he was ordered. He looked to be balancing the amount of

many against his own brother's life.   With his gun
still pointing at Jack, Trey conceded and dropped the
case of money.   Then something peculiar took
place.   Trey reached into his pocket and made a
phone call.   The only words he spoke were,   "Kill
the bitch now."

From behind a building, Tony had managed
to sneak around toward Caroline as   she kept her
gun trained on Little Chief.   From his vantage point,
he had a good chance at making his target.   Caroline
was in his sights and there was little she could do.

"Just say when, boss."   Tony said,
boastfully.

"Do it and you all die right here right now,
starting with you."   Jack was now pointing his gun
at Trey.   Appearing to be a Mexican stand off, only
suicide would prevail in such a situation.   And then
it happened.   All at once, and totally unexpectedly.
A shot rang out, loud and certain.   The echo
between the buildings was deafening.   No one could
discern who had fired the first shot, or at whom.
And then it finally became obvious.   His arm
dropped first, but he managed, somehow, to remain
on his feet as he staggered into the middle of the
street.   His gun was still firmly harbored in his
grasp.   Looking like something extremely horrid
from a zombie movie, he dragged one foot in front of
the other, kicking up dirt and dust with his eyes
already rolled up in his head.   As he rigidly scuffed
his feet further, all who were close enough could see
that nearly half his head had been blown off from
behind the ears.   He fired his gun into the ground
narrowly missing his own feet as he dragged himself
a few yards further.   And as he bled-out, he teetered
forward and collapsed in a bellowing cloud of dust.
Tony was dead.   And the one responsible for his
demise was yet to be discovered until she finally

appeared from behind the building.   Showing signs of weakness, she managed to use the side of the building for balance as she ambled slowly to view. With her weapon still in hand, she raised her arm, pointing the pistol at Trey.   Somehow Crystal had managed to save Caroline's life by taking out the ace in the hole that Trey was, obviously, relying on.   His vengeance on the one who killed his little brother would not be played out as planned.   Crystal took cover behind a car, taking steady aim and keeping her balance by leaning on the hood of a car.

The sudden silence was deafening.   All eyes were on Trey.   It was his move.   The look of pure evil in his eyes was a stunning family resemblance.

During all the commotion, no one had noticed that Little Chief had managed to free his hands from the duct tape that had previously bound him. Caroline was keeping steady aim at Trey ever since the lead thug decided to train his gun at Jack. Protecting her husband became her instinctive priority.

Though the odds were in Jack's favor, he didn't want to take the chance of an all out war.   He got his daughter back, and they got the money back as an extra bonus.   The last thing he would have wanted was to see the last man standing.   Too many family members would get hurt.   And Jack was not the gambling type.   His way of dealing with business was always with assured guarantees.   Even with his father and Roberto up on the rooftop of the building poised to take out the enemy with their riffles, Jack knew it wasn't their way of conducting business.   Furthermore, Jack also knew that the highest reward would payout in ample dividends if one of the thugs managed to hurt or kill his wife. And knowing that Carline would be the first target, Jack made every effort to alleviate the stress that was falling upon Trey's shoulders. "It looks like Tony wont be able to make it for dinner tonight, pal. Perhaps you and the rest of your posse should consider the fact you wont make it out of here in any better shape if you don't leave here now…while you can." Jack was lenient with his words, but never showing any weakness.

Suddenly, the look in Trey's face changed from despair to a glimmer of hope. At first, Jack and those who were close enough to see, might have thought that Trey simply decided to shoot it out and hope for the best. But that wasn't the case. Evident to Trey, but no one else, was Little Chief who had risen to his feet and managed to get the jump on Caroline. When Jack was delivering his speech to Trey, Little Chief was busy making a silent approach towards Caroline. Disregarding the basic fundamentals of combat, Little Chief came up behind Caroline and managed to put her into a suffocating chokehold. Immediately, she reacted in a defensive maneuver. She stomped her foot into his shin, sliding the hardened heal of her boot down to his foot. Though the maneuver had to be painful for the thug, he managed to keep his hold on her neck. Caroline was no match for his strength. Nor would she be able to achieve a rollover flip maneuver. As her air reserves were running thin fast, she did as any good soldier would do and shot a hole in Little Chiefs right foot. Once she was released, she gasped and struggle to gain back her aplomb.

The obscenities and vulgar language was just the beginning of Little Chief's rant. As he hobbled and crouched while trying to stop the bleeding, he pleaded and begged for his brother to shoot Caroline. "What are you waiting for, bro. Shoot the damn bitch! She took out our brother…man. What are you waiting for?" Calling out his derogatory commands, Little Chief continued to writhe in pain. "Give me a damn gun, somebody, and I will do it." Little Chief looked around with open arms and bloodied hands, searching for anyone who would throw him a gun.   Finally, one proud thug decided to be a hero.   He was the closest to Little Chief. No sooner the young minion tossed a gun to his second in command, a rifle shot sounded from the rooftop.   The young soldier was dead before his face hit the dirt.   The Uzi landed fifteen feet short of Little Chief's reach.

Caroline knew it was her job to keep him from getting the gun, but she didn't dare expose herself from behind her position of safety.   Any one of the thugs would have gladly taken her out if they had the chance.   "Don't even think about it, Little Prick."   Caroline warned as Little Chief, slowly made his way toward the gun.   "Last warning…"

"Fuck you, bitch!"   Little Chief angrily snarled.

"Funny, that's exactly what your brother said…just before I turned his head inside out." Caroline knew her psychological tactics were working well on him.   Getting him angry made her job much easier.   He wasn't the type who could work proficiently while under tress and pressure.

"We'll see who dies next…"   Little Chief made his way to the gun.   He stood over it while facing Caroline.   The challenge was on.   He looked at the gun and back at Caroline.   In his mind, he was doing the math and measuring the distance between.

"What are you waiting for, Little Dick?" Caroline yelled loud enough for all to hear.   Her insults were driving a huge hole in the man's ego, big enough to drive a truck through.   "Hurry up and get dead already.   I haven't had breakfast."

"You fucking bitch…"   Little Chief growled.

Taking one last judgment glance, he strategically dropped to his knees and then onto his chest and gained control over the Uzi rather quickly.   Rolling to one side as if she were attempting a military maneuver, he was already too late to take aim.

Caroline fired three shots into his face, using his nose as the center target.   Much like the hours spent at shooting range, Caroline was an above average marksman.   Immediately after shooting Little Chief dead were he lay, Caroline pivoted and took aim at Trey, firing off one more round.   In the act of shooting at Little Chief, she took no chances, believing that the hail of fire would have already started soon after she fired her first round at his brother.

But Trey never moved, not even after the slug hit him in the left shoulder.   He seemed to be in shock after seeing his brother killed right in front of him.   "My face will be the last thing you will ever see when I kill you, bitch."   Trey was fuming with unspent energy and anger.

"I guess you will have to stand in line then, Ugly Fuck or Big Pimple or whatever stupid handle you go by.   It's all the same to me.   Just bring it on already…I'm tired of your bullshit…let's go!"   She shouted, doing her best to get his goat, throw him off his game and cause him to make a critical mistake just as his two brothers did.

Just as Caroline was making progress with her psychological warfare, a handful of the resident Indians had come down from the hills with seventeen captives all tied and bound walking toward the center of town in single file.

"There will be no more blood letting on this land."   Johnny Whitefeather called out as he delivered the thugs to Trey.   "I believe these trespassers belong to you."   Johnny smirked as he looked Trey in the eyes with a nasty smirk. "If you want the rest of the bodies from up there, you're going to have to collect them yourself. I'm not your fucking maid, dawg." Johnny announced as five tribal police trucks pulled up with a dozen more armed officers.

"Like I said before, you best leave here now, while you can…while you are able." Jack instructed. "I think you have caused yourself enough trouble."

Johnny turned to Trey one last time. "And clean up this mess before you leave." Johnny pointed to Trey's dead brother and Tony's body.

As infuriated as Trey may have been, he knew he was outnumbered and fighting a futile battle. There was little he could do to redeem his name and rank. As he gave the command to his drones to collect the bodies and untie the captives, he made one last announcement. "This aint over…" Trey's snarling words were directed at Caroline specifically.

Caroline showed no fear when making her reply. "With Big Mike it simply was business…with you, it became personal when you took my daughter. Name the time and place, Little Pecker and I will be happy to accommodate you and *all* your high school dropouts. Oh, but next time, try to leave the children out of it. Such a cowardice act is really unbecoming. Not that you or your flunkies would know from real bravery." Caroline was relentless with the personal insults. She really wanted it to end then and there. The idea of looking over her shoulder for the rest of her life was not her idea of   pleasant tranquility. It would have been so much easier if he tried anything suspicious so she could have blown him away. No doubt, without him, the worker-drones and thugs would have disbanded and given up the fight, and all worries would have dissipated in the breeze.

Chapter Twenty-six
Recovery

Just before the showdown, Crystal was gaining back her strength slowly, at least enough to hear when Tony was sneaking around the back of the building she was resting in.   Upon her investigation, she found the young man working his way closer to Caroline.   Finding it evident that he was planning on causing her harm, Crystal knew that Pauly was right all along when he first fired him, and demoted him to a lesser paying position with the family. Thankfully, Tony was never privy to the more pertinent strategies and information leading to the eventual demise of Little Chief.

Soon after the last of the hoodlums had loaded their dead and left the reservation did anyone stand down their guard.   Thankfully, many of the native Indians on the reservation took pleasure in rounding up the novice warriors that were found lingering around the land in search of a vantage point.   However, Jack's crew took no prisoners.   It probably had been days before, Trey actually learned of his total casualty count, including Reno.   If nothing else, Caroline understood that it would take quite some time for him to gather and recruit enough forces to attempt another act against the family. Slow but surely, every last hoodlum was escorted from the reservation. Many of the tribal police stood guard at the front gate anticipating a return for revenge. Fortunately, that never happened.

After the street was finally clear, Crystal quietly found her way over to Caroline.   While heading to sit on the tailgate of an old truck, Crystal took Caroline by the hand and gave her a hug.   "It's over for now, honey.   You can remove the round from the chamber."   She said, calmly allowing for some reprieve.   "You did good, little sister.   I'm real proud of you."   Truly, such accolades coming from her were special and sincere.   "You almost got him with the *'Ugly Fuck'* name.   I thought for sure he was going to pop his cork on that one.   But I especially enjoyed the *'Big Pimple'*…yep, that one was my favorite."   Crystal could feel the warrior's anxiety still rushing through Caroline's pulsing veins.

Certainly, Caroline *was* still swimming in an ocean of adrenalin.   It seemed everyone, deep inside, wanted Trey to *'pop his cork'*.   But if he had, there was no telling who might have lost their life that day.   "He's right you know?"   Caroline commented with remorse.

Crystal tipped her head in answer, waiting for an elaboration.

"It's not over, not yet."   Caroline said, looking over toward the road hoping Jack would hurry back to her after checking the perimeter to make sure the thugs were gone.

"That's true, it's not over."   Crystal remarked matter of fact.   "But we all lived another day, to fight another day, *and* your baby is safe."

Caroline's face flushed with new color the moment Crystal mentioned El.   "Where is she?"

Crystal slipped her bottom off the tailgate of the car, and took Caroline by the hand toward, Sara's house.   "She's safe.   Come, I'll show you.   Of course, you may want to holster that first, sweetie." Crystal said, pointing to the Glock.

The girls entered Sara's house to find two of the crew standing guard over a concealed basement door.   Caroline tucked the gun back in the small of her back after ejecting the magazine and the round from the chamber.   Once Crystal announced the coast was clear, the two men pulled away the large rug that covered the entrance to the basement.   One of the guys reached for the hidden latch to unlock the door, while the other helped to lift the heavy wooden floorboard that doubled as a door.   Inside, were Sara and two more of Pauly's crew members standing guard with Little El who looked amazing for someone who had been kidnapped.   Once the stairs were put into place, Little El climbed up and exited the basement with open arms for her mom.   The bravest one in the room appeared to be El as everyone else was nearly in tears watching the reunion.   After all that had taken place that day, it was an amazing miracle no one from the family got hurt.

Little El caught a glimpse of her daddy coming in the door of the house.   "Daddy!"   She shouted, urging him to come and hug the two of them.

"How are you, El?"   Jack said as he knelt down to her level while briefly looking her over.

"I'm fine, Daddy.   They didn't hurt me." Her cheery disposition was untainted and as happy as ever.

Jack whisked her up in his arms, and gave her a kiss on the cheek while hugging them both. Taking a deep, respiring breath, he held them tightly, assuring them both an impenetrable security. "I'm glad to hear that."   Jack looked to Caroline.   "And you?"   Jack planted a kiss on her forehead.

"Still stewing and processing it all.   But I'm, otherwise,   fine."   Caroline reported confidently.

"Finest soldier I have seen in a long time." Crystal added as both Pauly and Roberto came into the house.

"Where did you find this one, Jack?"   Pauly asked referring to Caroline and her spunky, antagonizing nature.   "That Trey fellow is going to need some serious therapy after today, I tell ya." Pauly found it rather humorous that Caroline would choose to be so bold and insulting to Trey.

"Yeah, it'll take him at least two years just to relocate his manhood."   Roberto added.   "Good job, sis.   Remind me, next time I need a head shrink or a lesson in humility, I'll just call on you." Roberto and the rest of them had a good laugh, now that it was finally over.

Pauly made a personal effort to check on Caroline, making sure she was okay and not too shook up.   "We're all very proud of you.   You did well out there."   Pauly commended, patting her on the back.

"Thank you, Pauly.   I appreciate that."   Her calm demeanor was hiding something deeper though.

Pauly picked up on it right away.   "Whatever it is you have on your mind right now, we will take care of it, I promise."   Pauly said, offering a wink, so not to say too much in front of El.

"The sooner, the better…"   Caroline added.

Pauly and Roberto both nodded.   "Perhaps, but we will talk about that later.   Right now, we are going to order about fifty of sixty pepperoni pizzas and have some fun.   Tomorrow is my granddaughter's birthday and it starts today."   Pauly announced adding some elated cheer to the room.

"Yay!!!"   Little El chimed in as Pauly took hold of her, dancing her around the room like the silly grandfather he enjoyed portraying.   While Pauly paraded around the room dancing and frolicking about, he had purposely allowed for Mom and Dad to talk privately.

"I'll be right back, baby."   Caroline announced to her daughter as Jack was leading her outside to the porch.

"Okay, Mommy."   El giggled as Grandpa continued to dance in a playful and silly manner, spinning her around and dipping her.

Jack and Caroline stepped outside, closing the door behind them.   Making the first move, she wrapped her arms around her man with an unrelenting hold.   The wound-up tension in her body could probably have been felt from a block or two away.   "I know just what you are thinking, but believe me, we will take care of this at a more opportune time."   Jack opened the conversation, knowing her fears and concerns.

"I just wish it was over now, and not later." Caroline opened up with her honesty.

"I get that, but the situation was too dangerous, especially for you.   I wasn't about to take that chance.   We have eyes in the sky as we speak, and plenty on new intel coming in every minute.   Besides, the logistics with so many bodies would not have made my job very easy.   The best strategy is to let their people handle their dead and wounded…and when the time is right, we strike the lead guy when he is alone and least expecting it. You of all people should know warfare should not be a gamble or chance predictions.   A good defense is great, but a precision and perfected offence is even better."   Jack reasoned. His knowledge and expertise in such matters certainly garnered the respect he deserved.

"I know what you are saying is right and I feel it in my heart that you and your crew know best, but I still feel the threat is too risking having let him go like we did.   He wont stop, not until he has hurt El."   She said, claiming what she felt in her soul.

"For one, he will never get the chance to get close enough to her.   And two, you need to allow me to work my end of things.   You may not like what I do for a living, but the reality is, I do my job well and we work as a family.   Now, Dad and I have already been discussing your involvement in the business--"   Jack wasn't pulling any punches.

"And you think I will join you…willingly?" Caroline was only seeing the worst aspect of things.

"Let me finish what I was about to say.   Our order of business will be locating Trey and finding his most vulnerabilities.   Then you and I take him out, together, as a team with organization and precision."   Jack said, making his point quite clear.

"That part of business sounds feasible.   I'm

just not keen on the other part of your business."
She reported, feeling she might have opened a can of
worms.

"And that makes sense considering what you
saw, and not knowing the reasons behind it." Jack
allowed for the worms to escape. "What you saw
was the utmost dregs of my work. If you could
imagine walking in on your execution of Little Chief,
one might think you were equally unreasonable in
your actions. And yet, your actions, in your eyes
and everyone else, were fully condoned by all, and
found to be righteously appropriate. What you
walked in on that one day and witnessed was as big
as, if not bigger, a threat to the family…"

"But the children, Jack? Really?" Caroline
made her point clear as her eyes were livid and
unrelenting with a defending cause.

"I had a rough time with it too, Caroline. I
don't doubt that was why you showed up at my place
of work, sensing my depression and discomfort with
the job. Unfortunately, the children were collateral
damage that could not be avoided. Believe me
when I tell you, that was the first and last time any
such thing had happened. We had a, one time,
window of opportunity, and I took it. I wasn't
happy about it, and I certainly didn't enjoy my job
that day. Obviously, you detected my depression
prior to the job, and I apologize for that. But
business must go on, no matter how much we may
disagree with the details. If such a task could have
been avoided, we would have taken the alternative
rout. By acting as I did that day, we averted the
deaths of many. We also sent an overt message to
those who might sympathize with his cause. The
de-rooting and execution of the family was a
necessary means to an end." Jack wasn't backing
down. It was important that Caroline see just how

important his role in the family business actually was. Surely, politics can be rather ugly.   The aftermath of any war-torn scenario will have its share of ugliness. Time and time again, history has revealed plenty of unsavory images.   But the fact remained, Jack had an important job to do.   And by conducting his work accordingly, he managed to avert a war between two very powerful families.

"I understand.   I just don't like it." Caroline subdued her protest.   "I hope never to have to see such a thing again."

"Does this mean what I hope it means?" Jack wasn't wasting any time with his inquiries.   He had gone far too long not knowing his place with his wife and child.

"As much as I don't like certain aspects of your job, I can't live another day without you in my life."   She conceded with yearning desires.

Crystal had her ear to the door, listening in on the conversation.   She gave thumbs up to Pauly and Roberto as she eavesdropped.

"You have no idea how happy that makes me."   Jack reached for his girl, pulling her in his arms, he hugged her with every loving part of his soul.

"Oh, I think I might."   Caroline added.

Part II -- 'Out of Range'
Chapter Twenty-seven
Training

After Jack and Caroline went back inside Sara's house, it was discovered that everyone inside already knew of the exciting news, but held out to hear it from the couple.   A hushing silence fell over the room as they came back into the house.   It looked as though an announcement was warranted as the silence and stares grew more intense.   Hand in hand the two looked rather happy considering all the havoc that occurred that day.   Jack stepped up and made his speech.   "Caroline is staying."

"Always talking too much, Jack."   Crystal joked.   "And how do you feel about us now, Caroline?"

Caroline thought a moment, thinking how deep the question was.   "I have always loved all of you.   My decision to leave was a personal conviction that I had a great deal of trouble getting past.   I was scared and confused at the time we separated.   I'm still not completely sold on the idea of how business operates with the family, but I think that is something I will have to work with.   I have come to learn that I have a family that loves me unconditionally.   I have a husband who loves me more than life itself, a daughter who loves her daddy very much.   And I have an endless love for my husband who means the world to me as well.   I know it's not going to be an easy road to travel, but I would rather travel the road with my entire family than have to face another day alone without all of you in my life.

Pauly initiated the applause that lasted long enough for Crystal to think of a speech of her own. "And on that note, we would like to assure you that you are never alone in any matter.   You can come to me or Pauly anytime you feel you need an ear to talk to.   The family business can be a bit overwhelming at given times.   We all understand that.   But that's why we have each other to communicate with, to resolve our differences and discuss our opinions or fears.   I was there too, Caroline, right where you are now.   It wasn't easy for me either, but family is worth the time to reason and consult.   I think you will find that we are not as different as you first thought, little sister.   And after the performance we all saw out there on the street, I have a feeling you are a natural at protecting your family and what is yours."

"Here, here…"   Pauly raised a bottle of flavored water for cheer and a toast.   "To the little warrior who could!   Salute."

Once all the speeches were out of the way and

the pizzas were delivered and devoured, everyone seemed to settle down from the action that took place earlier in the day.   Many of the native residents that participated in the round up joined in the festivities as well.

Though Caroline never got to meet with Jason inasmuch as he had left long before the ruckus broke out, she felt the effects of his presence.   Crystal had made it clear to everyone that he had, in deed, saved her life.   Her condition took several hours to show a positive change, but the change continued to improve with every passing hour.   Everyone who saw her suffering and withering away prior to the treatment could clearly see the improvement and the exponential changes in her.   It truly was a miracle to be seen.

The entire family and all crew members stayed the night, camped out in their cars, some bunked up with the local residence, while others stayed awake keeping vigil for intruders.

Caroline took a particular interest in her new found friend, Sara.   The three girls, Caroline, Crystal and Sara, stuck together closely talking about the Indian culture and how similar Pauly's family beliefs actually were to that of their own.

When night came, so did the exhaustion. Caroline was suffering from nearly three days sleep deprivation, and Crystal was plain worn out from being miserably sick during the past six months. The girls including Little El all slept in Sara's house that night while the boys made do, roughing it as best they could where they could.

The following day was a different story. The plan was to make haste and trek back home as quickly as possible with as few stops as possible. Fortunately, the trip went well without a hitch.

Do to the fact that the drive had taken up most

of the day, plans were made to postpone El's birthday celebration until the following day when all her cousins could come and celebrate along with her. As adorable as El presented herself to be with little effort, she claimed that all she wanted for her birthday was to be with her mom and dad, together. El got her wish.   And the party was celebrated at her grandpa Pauly's house with all the family.   More speeches were made, and Caroline showed her gratitude for such wonderful family support.   Of course, the real celebration between Caroline and Jack didn't start until the evening they were back home together in their own bed.   It was a long awaited reunion.   Hopefully, their fun and laughter didn't keep El awake all night.

Surprisingly, it didn't take much but a couple of simple phone calls to seal up her life in Florida. Once she had concluded the calls, it was like the closure of a chapter was already in effect and the past was soon to be forgotten with her life picking up where she left off with Jack.

Just two days after Caroline's return, Jack had been doing his homework intensively.   Between the intel from the eye in the sky and the information gathered by investigators, Jack and his dad had accumulated enough information to formulate a concluding plan.   Much to Caroline's surprise, there would be no confrontation.   There would be no words exchanged between warriors.   The time for insults and frontal assaults was over.   The time for emasculating thugs had long passed.   A stealthy single shot from a sniper rifle was all it took to take Trey out on the front porch of his own home.   A single round struck him, killing him instantly, seconds before the sound would report from where. The threat was over, and the worry subsided.   And the police investigation never reported any viable leads.

Incidentally, the cell phone used by Caroline and Jack for the ransom drop was placed on the front porch at Trey's feet. It was the last thing he would see before taking his last breath.

The end of part 2.
Part 3 is Out Of Range.

This book is a work of fiction.   Names, characters, places and incidences are products of the author's imagination or are used fictitiously.   Any resemblance to actual events or locales or persons, living or dead, is entirely coincidental.

Special thanks to Janette, my wonderful wife, for going far above and beyond the call of duty.   You make it all worth while.   I love you very much.

Volumes of gratitude to the Ronald McDonald house of Loma Linda, California. Please, give generously to such a wonderful cause.

THANK YOU FOR SAVING MY SON'S LIFE, Loma Linda Children's Hospital of Loma Linda, California.

Thank you with all my heart, literally, to Loma Linda International Heart Institute.

Special acknowledgement to Robert Dunn author of: Invasion of Long Beach, Long Beach Nights, Flawed From Inception, A Killing in The Market, Sowing in The Morning, Whispers of a Secret God, Houser Pride of America, and Proverbs of Solomon.

First and second phase editing by J. Myers and C. Dunn.

Special thanks to Janette and her family for making it possible for me to continue writing considering all my health issues.

K S Michaels has also authored;
Love Returns Through the Portal of Time
Love's Eclipse of The Heart
Love That Transcends Time
When To Give Up On Life And Child,
My Near Death Experience
Philosophy The Obsession
Erotica, Fantasy By Numbers Volume 1
Out Of Justice
Then Came The Lightning
Erotica, Fantasy by numbers Volume 2
Out Of Revenge
Then Came The Thunder
Out Of Range
Out Of The Blue
The Self Rescue Manual
Out Of Bounds

K S Michaels is a survivor of over twenty-nine heart surgeries due to a rare congenital heart disease.   He is a doting husband and a proud daddy.   When not writing novels, he spends much of his donated time as a motivational speaker helping parents of behaviorally challenged adolescent children, and victims of the chronically ill at various hospitals and colleges.   He offers accolades to Loma Linda International Heart Institute and Long Beach Memorial hospital for saving his life on more than one occasion.   He grew up in Woodland Hills California, and presently resides in the High Desert of California.   His Autobiography is titled: *'When To Give Up On Life And Child'*

Author contact: kiowazranch@yahoo.com or P O Box 294846, Phelan California 92329